Mistletoe for Felicity

Mistletoe for Felicity

A REGENCY ROMANCE

SALLY BRITTON

For Marti & The Cottage
A New Friend for Christmas

One

DECEMBER 1ST, 1816

T he quaint London church was silent except for the vicar's voice, which echoed through the hallowed space. Felicity stood beside her soon-to-be husband, the weight of her decision heavy in her heart as she listened, with only half her awareness, to the words being recited.

Her gaze flitted over the limited gathering—her late-grandmother's friends, most likely attending out of a sense of duty to her memory as none of them had connection to Felicity beyond that. Her grandmother's solicitor stood a little apart from the others, a neutral observer of the proceedings. It was he who had brought the proposal to her, acting on behalf of the merchants, *Mr. Samuel Harcourt and Son.*

Today, she married the son. Whose name was Theodore.

The offer of marriage had been a shock, a rescue line thrown to her when she'd believed herself destined to face the world without a protector. Though her father had been an earl, his heir was a complete stranger to her. A distant cousin, who had suffered her grandmother and Felicity to live in a dower house on his estate. But ten months ago, Grandmother also passed away, and the earl had told Felicity he wanted her to move on as soon as possible. And while her modest inheritance made taking rooms somewhere far from London a possibility, the funds didn't offer her what a woman needed most in the world of men: protection.

She risked a glance at her groom and clutched her bouquet tighter, the small white blooms a stark contrast against the dark fabric of her dress.

Am I doing the right thing? she wondered, her heart fluttering in her chest. Grandmother's solicitor had assured her he'd found nothing in her groom's background or associations to cause alarm.

The way he had greeted her that morning, with a respectful nod and a faint smile, had reassured her. Until the moment their shoulders had brushed during the morning sermon. He'd stiffened and moved slightly away from her, creating several inches of space between them.

Perhaps he was only nervous.

His chiseled jaw, strong profile, and the dark locks that brushed his forehead marked him as undeniably handsome. His stance, though rigid, did not radiate coldness. Had she seen kindness in his eyes? Or merely politeness? His composed demeanor and the gentle way he had offered her his arm to escort her to the front of the church hinted at a man capable of respect, making her hope fervently that her instincts were right.

Her dreams for their future were simple yet profound: kindness, comfort, warmth, laughter, and understanding. She envisioned cozy evenings by the fire, shared books, whispered conversations, and perhaps even the soft patter of little feet on wooden floors. The thought of children made her heart ache sweetly.

She realized they had come to that very part in the ceremony, and she struggled to listen intently.

" . . . reverently, discreetly, advisedly, soberly, and in the fear of God; duly considering the causes for which matrimony was ordained. First, it was ordained for the procreation of children, to be brought up in the fear and nurture of the Lord, and to the praise of his holy name."

As an only child, her solitary games often made her yearn for companionship that only siblings could provide. The hope that she might one day be surrounded by the lively chatter and innocent mirth of children was a deeply cherished one.

The vicar's words took up her entire attention at last, as he asked his final question of her almost-husband. "Wilt thou love her, comfort her, honor, and keep her, in sickness and in health; and, forsaking all other, keep thee only unto her, so long as ye both shall live?"

Mr. Theodore Harcourt answered without hesitation, with a firmness that made her heart stutter. "I will."

Then it was her turn.

"Wilt thou obey him, and serve him, love, honor, and keep him, in sickness and in health; and, forsaking all other, keep thee only unto him, so long as ye both shall live?" The vicar looked at Felicity with a probing gaze, prompting her for the final affirmation.

"I will." Felicity's voice, when it emerged, was clear and steady, filled with hope for all the tomorrows that lay ahead.

TAD FELT AN UNCHARACTERISTIC KNOT OF ANXIETY IN his stomach. Standing there at the front of the intimate gathering, on his wedding day, his eyes kept drifting back to the woman beside him. She was undeniably beautiful, with an air of grace and a spark of determination in her eyes that he had immediately noticed when they briefly met the day before.

How did Father manage this? he thought, not for the first time. A woman like Felicity, both willing and unattached, seemed almost too good to be true. Their union had been arranged with a swiftness that made Tad's head spin, and while he felt a twinge of gratitude to his father for organizing the match, he was also deeply uneasy.

His life, until this point, had been consumed with the intricate dealings of the family business. The smell of ink and the heft of ledgers were as familiar to him as his own heartbeat. He feared the void that would emerge with the absence of daily business interactions. Questions of his new lot in life yet gnawed at him, casting a deeper shadow on his unease.

Was he ready to become a gentleman? Could he find purpose in a role that was so entirely unfamiliar to him? The term 'gentleman' was now his new reality, yet its true meaning felt distant and obscure, wrapped in vague notions of leisure and privilege. Would he find satisfaction in a life so removed from the hands-on toil and labor that had once defined him?

The mere thought of living such a life unraveled a tapestry that had once been so familiar, leaving threads of his past disconnected from the fabric of his future, and it filled him with a sense of discomfort.

Tad's gaze slid to Felicity once more. Would she find him interesting enough? The fear of being perceived as dull and unadventurous plagued him. After all, he was a man used to routine, to facts and figures. Didn't women wish for someone who could make their heart race? Someone capable of romantic musings and a commanding presence?

A memory rose unbidden, of his father's stern voice echoing

through the wood-paneled study of their townhouse. "Duty to the family, Theodore, that comes first. Always."

The weight of expectation bore down on him. He didn't want to let his family down, and the added responsibility of caring for a wife amplified his worries.

The vicar's voice became clear again, breaking Tad's trail of thoughts. It was time for his vows. He gave them with all the sincerity he could muster, hoping against hope that this unfamiliar path would lead to happiness for both him and the lady beside him.

Tad slid a thin gold band around her delicate finger, swallowing at how small her hand was, how pale, compared to his own square palm and sun-darkened skin. Perhaps he'd spent too much time on the docks.

"Forasmuch as Theodore and Felicity have consented together in holy wedlock, and have witnessed the same before God and this company, and thereto have given and pledged their troth either to other, and have declared the same by giving and receiving of a ring, and by joining of hands; I pronounce that they be man and wife together, In the Name of the Father, and of the Son, and of the Holy Ghost. Amen."

At last, the formalities of joining two people came to an end.

Outside the church, the early winter air was brisk, carrying with it the scent of impending snow. Tad's mother, with a grace that had always reminded him of a delicate bird, gently took Felicity's hand in hers.

"I'm so pleased to finally have a daughter-in-law," she said, her voice warm, her eyes even warmer. "We will be sure to visit once you two are settled."

"Perhaps—perhaps at Christmas?" his new bride ventured with a sweet shyness that made him smile.

His mother's brow furrowed, though her expression

remained pleasant. "Perhaps. We shall see."

Tad saw Felicity's grateful nod and the light blush that stained her cheeks. She drifted a few steps away from him to greet an elderly woman. Very few people had attended the service, and fewer still had remained to wish the two of them a happy journey. Had his bride avoided telling her friends of their union? He'd seen no ladies near her age in attendance.

His father's firm hand on his shoulder pulled him from his observations. Meeting the older man's gaze, Tad saw a flicker of approval in Harcourt Senior's dark eyes.

"This is a new start for all of us, Tad," his father murmured. "And a new world for you." The few words were laden with unsaid emotions, and Tad merely nodded, the weight of his responsibilities and the magnitude of the day pressing heavily on him.

As Tad approached his bride to escort her to the waiting carriage, a gentleman dressed in fine clothing and wearing a smug smile bowed over her hand.

"You make a beautiful bride, my lady. May your days be brighter than those in the past," the man said, voice pitched so low that Tad barely heard him as he stopped at his wife's side.

"Thank you, Lord William," she said in return, curtseying. "It was kind of you to come." Then she looked up at Tad. Her cheeks turned a slight shade of pink.

"I must be on my way," the lord said, then tipped his hat to Tad before striding in the opposite direction from the newly-weds. Avoiding an introduction, perhaps.

It wasn't the first time Tad had experienced prejudice from nobility. He ignored the slight and extended his arm to his wife. "It is time to leave."

"Already?" Her lips tilted upward, the sight of even her hesitant smile somewhat encouraging.

Helping Felicity into the carriage, Tad's hands fumbled slightly, a contrast to his usually deft movements. She had to pause, one foot on the step, until he steadied himself. Inside, the plush surroundings should've offered comfort, but instead, Tad felt the space closing in on him. He cleared his throat, sensing the need to fill the silence, yet unsure of where to start.

"I've . . . um, spent some time preparing the house for our arrival," he began hesitantly, the words not flowing as smoothly as he'd hoped. "It's a two-hour ride from here. I trust you're warm enough?" His eyes darted to the fur draped across her lap, a brief distraction from the storm of thoughts in his mind.

Felicity smiled gently, her voice soft and sweet when it came. "I am, thank you. And I'm eager to see our new home."

Home. Such a simple word carried so much weight. Tad nodded, stealing a glance out of the window, his own reflection staring back at him, showing the uncertainty he felt. The carriage's sharp movements underscored the rhythm of his racing heart.

Trying to find a subject that might ease the tension he felt, Tad ventured, "The estate I've purchased has a unique name. Its previous owners called it Winterway House." He hesitated, wondering how she'd react. "We can always rename it if you prefer something different."

Felicity looked thoughtful for a moment, a smile playing on her lips. "Winterway House," she repeated, savoring the words. "It's quite enchanting, actually. And it's a curious coincidence— it's reminiscent of my maiden name, Winters. Keeping the name would feel like a way to maintain a connection to my family. A bridge between my past and our future."

Tad folded his arms, tucking himself into the corner of the carriage. "I hadn't thought about the similarity. It's a happy coincidence, isn't it?"

She nodded. "It is. Perhaps it's a sign that all of this was meant to be, in its own strange way."

Her optimism shone brightly in her hazel eyes, and Tad found himself warming to it, albeit cautiously. It seemed that every word from her was a balm to his anxieties, even if just for a fleeting moment.

Felicity fidgeted with her gloves for a moment before hesitatingly offering, "Since we have a bit of a journey ahead, perhaps we could use this time to become better acquainted?"

Tad swallowed. Though precisely what he wanted, the thought still made him want to squirm. He hadn't spoken to many women of things other than surface-level topics, such as the weather and the health of their families. "Of course. That would be quite practical."

Encouraged, Felicity ventured her first question, "Do you have a favorite season?"

He pondered it a bit longer than necessary, suddenly conscious of how such simple questions could reveal so much. "Autumn, I suppose," he finally responded, "when the harvest comes in and the world is draped in shades of gold and red. It's a busy time for the family business, but also rewarding."

She gave him an encouraging smile. "That sounds lovely. And, if you don't mind my asking, do you have a favorite way to pass the time? What do you enjoy doing during your leisure hours?"

Caught slightly off guard, Tad cleared his throat. "Well, I've taken an interest in reading. I've also been partial to history and geography. And occasionally playing chess." He quickly added, realizing how mundane he must have sounded. His eyes darted to her fine gloves and the delicate way she held herself, every inch the lady. A pang of doubt gnawed at him. "But there hasn't been much leisure time. Not really. Business is always ... busy."

He winced at the inanity of his answer, acutely aware of the gap in their stations and their upbringings, and terrified that he might already have given offense. "I hope that I can find more refined pursuits befitting our new situation," he added, stumbling over the words, his face flushed.

She seemed to consider his words, her expression thoughtful. "I admire your dedication to your work. I hope you'll enjoy that you have more time now. Chess is such a complex game of strategy. I've always wanted to learn. Perhaps you could teach me?"

Tad's mouth fell open in surprise. "Yes. Of course. If you wish." Had he sounded too eager? He remembered he should reciprocate the questions she asked of him. "And you, Lady Felicity? Do you have a preferred season or pastime?"

Her eyes sparkled. "Winter, strangely enough, given our conversation about Winterway House. I love the crispness in the air, the sense of stillness. As for leisure pursuits, I enjoy painting and music. I've also been known to lose myself in novels, much to my grandmother's chagrin."

The carriage jolted over a rough patch in the road, momentarily interrupting their conversation. Felicity gasped and grabbed her bonnet, while Tad clasped the bench seat in both hands. They met each other's startled, wide eyes. Then she laughed, breaking the momentary tension.

Tad found himself smiling, but a knot of uncertainty stayed in his stomach. Her laughter was musical, her presence a comfort, but the difference in their stations loomed before him like an ocean to be crossed.

Would he ever truly manage such a crossing when the differences between them had been shaped by years of disparate upbringing and expectation? He hoped so, but as the carriage rolled on, he could not shake the nagging doubt that his ignorance of his new station might somehow fail her.

Two

Winterway House came into view, standing dignified amidst the vast expanse of its grounds. Though not the grandest of estates, its elegant structure and complex brickwork hailing from the mid-1700s gave it an undeniable charm. Three stories high with ivy creeping up its walls, large windows framed by shutters and a sloping roof dotted with chimneys, it was picturesque against the backdrop of the setting sun and gray winter sky.

Felicity's hope soared as she drank in the sight. The house, with its slightly worn edges and sparkling windows, had an inviting warmth to it. It seemed to beckon, promising comfort and new memories.

As the carriage pulled to a halt, the front door swung open to reveal the household staff arrayed in the expansive entry hall, lined up in neat order. Their expressions were a mix of curiosity and hopeful expectation.

Stepping into the house and her new life, Felicity, with Theodore by her side, made her way into the hall. Each servant stepped forward in turn to be introduced. The housekeeper, Mrs.

Bennet, with graying hair and a kind face, gave a deep curtsy. The butler, Mr. Jones, with a balding pate and an erect posture, bowed with precision. She met maids and footmen, the cook, and a young errand boy. Each greeted Felicity with a mixture of formality and warmth.

While Felicity's manner was gracious, her intent to make each individual feel seen and valued, she couldn't help but sense her husband's growing unease. His gaze darted around the entry hall, as though worried.

After the introductions, he took a hesitant step toward her. "I trust everything is to your liking?"

She placed a reassuring hand on his arm which immediately stiffened beneath her touch. "It's beautiful, Mr. Harcourt. Truly."

He exhaled, though his stance remained tense. "Let me show you to your quarters."

Following him up the grand staircase, then down a carpeted corridor, and up another staircase, they reached a set of double doors. He opened them with a flourish. The room that greeted her was bathed in shades of calming blue and pristine ivory, with delicate patterns on the drapes and upholstery. A large four-poster bed sat regally against one wall, its draperies adding an ethereal charm. The furniture was elegant and functional, and the room felt both fresh and timeless.

"Oh, Mr. Harcourt," she breathed, delight evident in her voice. "It's wonderful."

He seemed to swell with pride, pleased that his efforts had found favor. But then, hesitantly, he pointed to a discreet door on one side of the chamber. "That door leads to my quarters. For convenience," he added quickly, a blush coloring his cheeks.

A wave of understanding washed over her, and she too felt a blush rise to her cheeks. The implications of that connecting door were not lost on her. Their marriage, while beginning in businesslike fashion, did hold certain expectations and responsibilities.

Caught in her thoughts, and the quiet weight of the unsaid, she murmured, more to herself than to him, "A new beginning in every sense."

Her new husband cleared his throat. "For both of us. I assure you."

She raised her eyebrows at him. "Indeed. I don't suppose you have been a husband before, any more than I have been a wife. We will have to learn together." She had such hopes of growing with him, of forming a true connection. Perhaps it was silly. Maybe even naive. But she yearned for their match to be more than a convenient arrangement.

She walked to the door that adjoined their room and pulled it toward her, looking through it to his room. It mirrored hers, but the blues were darker, the furniture of heavier wood. The masculine to her feminine, she realized with a smile.

"There is a key," he said, voice softer. "To keep on your side of the door. It is in the drawer of your bureau."

Did he mean to say it was up to her, whether the door between their chambers opened in the evening?

Felicity turned to him, about to respond, when a quiet tap at the open door to the corridor took her attention. Looking over, she saw her maid, Clara, a familiar face from her grandmother's household. With her arrival, Theodore seemed eager to exit both room and conversation.

"I shall leave you in your maid's capable hands," he said, nodding towards the servant. "I hope you'll rest after the journey. I'll see you at dinner, Lady Felicity."

She blinked, caught off guard by his swift departure. "Oh, but that's still some hours away."

He hesitated for a moment, as if contemplating a response,

but then simply gave a nod and left the room. The soft click of the latch as the door closed behind him left a small silence in its wake.

Felicity let out a soft sigh, feeling a mix of disappointment and confusion. Clara, ever observant, gently approached her. "My lady, would you like some assistance settling in?"

Felicity smiled at her maid, grateful for the familiarity in her new environment. "Yes, Clara. Thank you."

As Felicity began to unpack and get comfortable, Clara chattered on, filling the room with her cheerful voice. "The house is ever so lovely, my lady. And the staff—they're all so kind. Many were retained from the previous owners, the Deerwoods."

"The Deerwoods?" Felicity's curiosity was piqued.

Clara nodded, taking a pile of dresses to the wardrobe. "Yes, Mr. and Mrs. Deerwood. An elderly couple, very loved by the townsfolk. It's said they took great care of everyone in the village, especially the children. The staff describes them in the warmest of words. One would think the couple something out of a fairy tale," Clara said with a twinkle in her eye.

Felicity chuckled at the comparison. "And where are they now?"

Clara shrugged. "Moved somewhere up north, from what I've heard. Just sold this estate and left. Said it was time for a change. But they left behind quite the legacy of warmth and goodwill."

The comment resonated with Felicity. In this moment, surrounded by unfamiliar walls, the thought of filling this house with love and laughter like the Deerwoods seemed both challenging and inviting. As the sun began its descent outside her window, painting the room in a warm, golden hue, Felicity felt a renewed determination.

Winterway House would the perfect place for new beginnings. She would make it so.

❄

THE SOFT GLOW FROM THE FIREPLACE ILLUMINATED THE room, casting flickering shadows over Tad's meticulously chosen attire. The deep blue jacket, the crisp, ivory shirt beneath, and the polished shoes—every detail was in its proper place. And yet, the most minor of all details, the unassuming wooden door that connected his chambers to Felicity's, became the center of his attention.

Every few moments, as he made the final touches to his appearance, he'd find his gaze drifting back to that door. The polished brass key that he'd told her of earlier, which now most likely rested snuggly in the lock, felt like a weight in his thoughts.

Would she understand the gesture? Was it too forward or presumptuous of him to come near such a sensitive topic so soon?

Sighing, he ran a hand through his hair, momentarily mussing the careful styling his valet had insisted upon. With ledgers, there was clarity. Numbers added up, or they didn't. But with Lady Felicity—his wife, he reminded himself—it was as if he'd opened a ledger written in a language he barely understood.

Temptation tugged at him, urging him to simply knock on that connecting door and check on her. But doubt lingered, as did the fear of appearing too eager to assume an intimacy with her that did not yet exist in any form.

Shaking his head as if to physically dispel his indecision, Tad approached his main door that led out to the corridor, casting one last glance at the connecting door. Taking a deep breath, he exited into the corridor and knocked on Lady Felicity's outer door. It seemed safer, but even as he waited for her to answer, he understood that every step mattered, no matter how tentative.

Tad's breath caught the moment Lady Felicity opened her door. She stood there, looking radiant in a gown the color of fresh pine needles, a shade that made the green in her hazel eyes glitter mesmerizingly. Curls tumbled delicately down her neck, creating a soft, golden frame around her face. The vision of her took him by surprise, and a nervous warmth spread through him.

"My lady," he murmured, swallowing hard, "You look . . . exquisite."

She blushed under his gaze, the rosiness spreading across her cheeks like the first hint of dawn. "Thank you, Mr. Harcourt. You look quite dashing yourself."

Trying to recover from the unexpected onslaught of emotions, he offered her his arm. She took it as though the movement was quite natural, her touch sending little jolts of electricity through him. They walked in companionable silence through the dim corridors, with only the soft flicker of candles to guide them. The subtle scent of roses and pine emanated from her, further distracting him.

When they reached the grand dining room, he couldn't help but note the vastness of the polished table, gleaming in the soft light from the chandeliers above. It struck him then, the contrast of this expansive table and the fact that only the two of them would be dining.

He guided her to one end, pulling out the chair for her. "My lady," he gestured for her to sit.

She glanced at the distance between their assigned seats, a fleeting expression of disappointment crossing her features. But she took her seat graciously, murmuring her thanks.

Tad then made his way to the opposite end. The distance from her provided a momentary relief from the storm of emotions he'd felt earlier, but it also gnawed at him, reminding him of their current unfamiliarity.

Dinner began with an air of formality, and the massive, polished table between them made the feeling more pronounced. Tad found himself watching her, noting her smiles at particular dishes. As the courses came and went, the length between them felt like a chasm. He wished to bridge it but didn't quite know how.

Felicity toyed with a sprig of rosemary on her plate.

He cleared his throat, awkwardly breaking the silence. "Do you like the room Mrs. Bennet prepared for you?"

She glanced up, meeting his gaze. "It's very pleasant, thank you."

"If there is anything you wish to change, please tell me. Or Mrs. Bennet. I thought the blue and ivory were rather soothing, but I know nothing of a woman's preferences."

Her face lit up with a warm smile. "Did you choose the colors yourself?"

He nodded, somewhat bewildered by her flash of enthusiasm.

"Oh, that makes it all the better. The colors are just perfect." She hesitated for a moment before adding, "I was hoping that perhaps tomorrow you could give me a tour of the whole house."

He paused, taken aback that she would seek his company. But then the weight of responsibility pressed down on him. "I have an appointment with the steward tomorrow morning. It's rather pressing. I need to go over the ledgers and accounts, ensure everything is in order." The words sounded stiff, even to his own ears.

Her lips curved into a small, understanding smile. But he told himself he imagined the shadow of disappointment in her eyes. "Of course, Mr. Harcourt. Business matters must be attended to."

"I'm certain Mrs. Bennet would be delighted to show you everything. And she knows more than I do about the house."

"Yes." She kept her gaze on her plate. "Of course."

They finished their meal in more silence, and when Tad couldn't stand it any longer, he stood. "Perhaps you would like to see the drawing room."

"Oh. Yes." She rose, too, replacing her gloves as she stood.

The drawing room, while elegantly decorated with plush furniture and finely detailed woodwork, held an air of chilliness. The fire crackled in the hearth, but its warmth hadn't yet penetrated the room.

Felicity, looking small and vulnerable, sat at the edge of the sofa, her arms wrapped around herself as she tried to absorb the warmth from the flames. Tad remained upright, the weight of his uncertainty grounding him to the spot. He felt torn—part of him yearned to approach and ensure she was warm, but a more cautious part kept him rooted, unsure of how to navigate this new intimacy.

Her gaze wandered around the room, perhaps in search of a distraction, then settled on the mantelpiece.

"Perhaps we could read a book together?" she suggested hesitantly, nodding towards a leather-bound volume that lay there.

Surprised by the suggestion, Tad immediately picked up the book. Opening its cover at random, he was met with lyrical verses of poetry. A sudden heat rose to his cheeks, betraying his discomfort.

"I must confess," he began, attempting a lighthearted chuckle, "I've never had much of a fondness for poetry."

Felicity's eyes held a twinkle of amusement. "That's all

right," she replied gently. "Perhaps you might grow to appreciate it."

He passed her the book, his fingers brushing against hers for a moment. "You're welcome to read it, Lady Felicity. Maybe you can share some verses that might change my mind."

She smiled, a hint of playfulness in her eyes, and began flipping through the pages. While the distance between them remained, there was a subtle shift in the room—a bridge beginning to form.

As Felicity leafed through the pages, her fingers gently caressing the edges, Tad couldn't help but watch the play of emotions across her face. Each page she turned seemed to invoke a different sentiment: curiosity, reflection, and at times, joy.

After a few moments, she paused, her gaze fixing on a particular poem. "Ah, John Donne," she murmured with appreciation. "Would you mind if I read one aloud?"

Tad nodded, intrigued. Despite his general aversion to poetry, he was curious to hear her read. Perhaps it was less about the poetry and more about the melody of her voice that he wanted to immerse himself in.

Clearing her throat slightly, Felicity began:

"Come live with me, and be my love,
And we will some new pleasures prove
Of golden sands, and crystal brooks,
With silken lines, and silver hooks."

As she read, Tad felt himself drawn into the rhythm of the words, the emotions they evoked, and the beauty of Felicity's voice. The room now seemed to hold a warmth that went beyond the flames of the hearth.

When she finished, she looked up to find Tad's gaze fixed on her, and he hoped she didn't feel uncomfortable. Had he been staring too intently? Too long? For a moment, they both remained silent, the weight of Donne's words hanging in the air between them.

"That was . . . quite beautiful," Tad finally admitted, his voice barely above a whisper.

Her lips curved into a gentle smile. "Poetry has a way of touching the soul, don't you think?"

He chuckled softly. "Perhaps you're right. Maybe there is more to poetry than I initially believed."

The soft crackle of the fire was the only sound in the room after she finished reading. She looked up at him, the light from the flames dancing in her eyes, casting them in a warm, inviting glow. Then she glanced meaningfully at the empty place on the cushion beside her, before returning her gaze to his.

"Come, sit beside me, Mr. Harcourt," Felicity suggested, her expression kind. "Perhaps you might like to try reading aloud? I assure you, it's not as daunting as it may seem."

Tad hesitated, finding himself torn between the desire to join her and the ever-present fear of the unfamiliar. "I'm not sure I'd be any good at it," he admitted, trying to sound lighthearted.

Her smile turned encouraging. "I promise, I'll enjoy anything you read."

Before he could gather the courage to move, his gaze flicked to the ornate clock on the mantel. The ticking seemed suddenly loud, echoing his heartbeat. He used the time as an excuse, ignoring a pang of guilt.

"It's grown quite late," he noted, not meeting her gaze.

She followed his line of sight to the clock, then looked back at him with a small, understanding smile. "I suppose it has." Did he detect a hint of disappointment in her voice, or was he only imagining it? She rose. "It has been a long day. Turning in now is for the best."

There was the slightest suggestion of a question in her words. He ignored it. Offering his arm without a word.

Inwardly, he chastised himself. *You're afraid of your own wife, Tad,* he thought bitterly. The realization stung, but before he could muster a response, the moment passed, and the weight of their new relationship pressed down on him once more.

He escorted her back through the semi-darkness of their home, guilt and nerves gnawing at his gut as they walked in silence. At her door, she put her hand on the latch before looking up at him, her cheeks dark with her blush.

"Should I expect to see you again this evening?" she asked, her voice sweet and low in the shadows. Enticing him to ignore the clawing uncertainty in his heart.

Tad couldn't bring himself to meet her eyes when she asked the question. A lump formed in his throat, his heart racing. The reality of their new relationship, the expectations of the society they were part of, all of it suddenly overwhelmed his thoughts.

"No, my lady." He hated how unsteady he sounded. "Best if we retire to our respective chambers tonight. There are many matters I need to attend to early in the morning. We both need our rest."

He could feel her studying him, searching for something in his expression. Her eyes held a mix of understanding and a trace of sadness. "I understand, Mr. Harcourt," she replied softly, the formality of his address hanging heavy in the air between them. "Sleep well."

He managed a small, tight smile, unable to find the words to respond. As she closed the door, he hesitated for a moment, feeling a sense of loss he couldn't quite define. He turned and made his way to his own chambers, the image of her standing at the door, looking radiant yet vulnerable, haunting him.

In the sanctuary of his own room, Tad allowed himself to

unravel, the facade of composure giving way to a torrent of conflicting emotions.

With a weary sigh, he undressed, his movements mechanical, his thoughts elsewhere. His mind kept rehearsing the evening, the moments when he'd felt a connection, a spark of something more, only to have it snuffed out by his own doubts and fears. He regretted not sitting beside her, not reading to her, not taking her hand, and not saying yes to her question. He'd allowed his fear to dictate his actions, and he'd missed an opportunity to truly connect.

He shook his head, frustration mounting. It was not fear, he told himself. It was caution, prudence. He was a man of reason, of logic. Emotions, especially those as potent and bewildering as love, were a territory yet uncharted. He needed time to understand, to navigate this new landscape. Surely, Felicity would understand that.

But as he lay in bed, staring at the shadowed ceiling, he couldn't shake the nagging doubt that crept into his thoughts. Had he been too distant, too cold? Was he failing her already, just as they were beginning their journey together?

Hours passed, and sleep remained elusive. His mind filled with questions and doubts. What did she truly think of him? What did she expect from him? Was he capable of being the husband she needed?

He found himself rising from the bed, drawn as if by an invisible force towards that connecting door. His hand hovered over the latch, uncertainty warring with longing. He could hear the soft rustle of the wind outside, the distant call of a lonely owl, but all else was silent.

Taking a steadying breath, he opened the door just a crack. Shocked when it proved unlocked. What was he to make of that? He peered into the dimly lit chamber beyond. The room was dark, but the banked embers cast enough of a glow for him to see the still, sleeping form of his bride.

A wave of relief washed over him, mingled with a pang of disappointment. She slept peacefully, the boundaries he had set not worrying her, even as he now questioned them.

Closing the door quietly, he returned to bed, but the restlessness remained. He realized, with a clarity that had eluded him earlier, that he wanted to know her. Truly know her. Not just as Lady Felicity, his wife in name, but as the woman who had captivated him from their first meeting with her grace, her intelligence, and her gentle strength.

As dawn began to paint the sky with hues of pink and gold, Tad made a silent vow. He would take the steps needed to bridge the distance between them, to explore the complex tapestry of emotions that bound them. He could learn to read the ledger of her heart, no matter how unfamiliar the language might seem.

And with that promise, a sense of peace settled over him, allowing him to drift into a fitful sleep. His dreams filled with the soft scent of roses and pine, the melody of poetry, and the image of a woman who had become the focus of his new life.

Three

DECEMBER 2ND

The morning sun was shy, hiding behind a thick curtain of clouds. The house, vast and filled with numerous doors and rooms, beckoned Felicity to explore. After the restrained dinner the night before and Theodore's sudden departure, she felt the need for a diversion. With every door she opened, she was met with echoes of the past, each whispering tales of old.

She found herself in front of a door on the third floor, at the far end of the corridor, that seemed different from the others, somehow. She studied the paneling, the bronze knob with its depiction of a pine tree, and she shook her head. The difference was in her mind, merely a fanciful notion.

Still. Curiosity, always her companion, urged her forward. The door protested with a creak, but it revealed a room with furniture still covered in thick white cloths to protect again dust. But what caught her eye was an old painting resting on an easel by the window.

She went to the curtains and threw them open, casting more light into the dim room, and throwing the painting into view.

She studied it with interest, leaning close to take in the subtle details.

The painting depicted the town they had briefly passed through the day before. Lynwood Hollow. The colors were muted, the buildings looked older, and the skies had an overcast hue, as though it might rain at any moment. Yet, there was a charm to it, an allure that made her feel a deep connection to the people who had come before her, bringing happiness to their community. Perhaps Mrs. Deerwood herself had created this depiction.

A soft draft came from the closed window, slinking like a cat around her waist and making her shiver. From the corner of her eye, she caught the lift of a piece of paper on a table, right beside the painting. A small pewter stag acted as a paperweight, with one hoof standing on the corner of the ivory sheet. The paper looked old, the edges slightly curled. The script was elegant but bold.

Please take care of our little village.

The weight of the note settled in her heart. It felt like a plea, an urgent request left behind. She removed the deer, then clutched the paper close. Had Mrs. Deerwood left the note for the new occupants of her home?

As Felicity studied the painting, the room around her faded, and her mind wandered. The previous night's events returned to her. Why had it stung when Theodore said he didn't like poetry? Why had his reluctance to sit close by, to share more about himself, hurt her? And that distance at the dinner table—it wasn't just physical.

She hadn't known him long, but she'd already formed an image in her heart of a kind, if reserved, man. She'd hoped for a bond to form quickly between them. Not just as husband and wife, but as friends. She had longed for companionship, ever since her lonesome childhood days.

She tried to reason with her feelings. After all, he was a stranger to her, as much as she was to him. But wasn't that the very crux of it? They were strangers, embarking on the most intimate journey two people could share. And instead of closing that gap with shared moments and mutual exploration, they hesitated.

The soft glow of the candles, the verses of poetry, their shared laughter—these could have been the beginnings of lovely memories. But each opportunity was met with hesitance from her new husband. Was he not curious about her, about them? Did he not long for a connection as she did?

It was too much to ask of a single day's acquaintance. Logically, she knew this.

Felicity's fingers traced the frame of the painting, her mind momentarily distracted by its beauty. But the heart, now stirred, refused to quiet down. She yearned to understand her husband, to be understood by him. She wanted more than politeness and decorum. She *needed* a connection.

She hoped more time would settle those things. But for now, the mystery of the painting and note would serve as a diversion. It was a tangible puzzle to solve, one she could grasp, unlike the mystery that was her relationship with Theodore. Her husband of but a single day.

The soft rustle of skirts signaled Mrs. Bennet's approach even before Felicity heard her voice.

"Oh, there you are, Lady Felicity," the housekeeper remarked, her voice imbued with warmth. "I thought I might find you exploring. This room hasn't seen much light for some time."

Felicity turned to face the older woman, feeling a bit like a child caught in mischief. "I hope I wasn't overstepping. I stumbled upon this room and was captivated by the painting."

Mrs. Bennet came closer, her gaze fondly resting on the artwork. "Ah, the view of our town. Mrs. Deerwood loved this piece dearly. If you're fond of it, we could have it moved to your chamber. It would fit perfectly above the hearth."

"That would be lovely, thank you," Felicity replied, appreciating the housekeeper's kind offer.

"You are mistress of this house, my lady. Anything you wish done, it will be done," the housekeeper reminded her with a gracious nod of her head.

Felicity's cheeks warmed. "Of course." She wasn't a guest. Or a younger relation. She was the mistress of this place.

As they exited the dimly lit room, Felicity's curiosity piqued again. "Mrs. Bennet, can you tell me more about Mrs. Deerwood? The painting gives the impression she had a deep connection with the village."

Mrs. Bennet smiled, her wrinkles deepening around her eyes as memories seemed to wash over her. "Mrs. Deerwood is an exceptional lady. A pillar of strength and kindness in this community. We all love her dearly. She has a heart that cherished both the grandeur of these halls and the simplest flower in on the village green. She often opened her heart and her home to the community."

Felicity's eyes widened with interest. "Did she host many events at Winterway?"

Mrs. Bennet nodded enthusiastically. "Indeed, she did. Winterway House was always alive with laughter and music during her time here. Every winter, a week before Christmas, she hosted a ball that the entire village looked forward to. And then on New Year's Day, there was another grand celebration."

Felicity's heart warmed at the thought. "It sounds as though Winterway House has seen many happy moments."

The housekeeper's face glowed with nostalgia. "Yes, Lady Felicity. And I have faith it will see many more under your care."

"That is most kind of you to say. Thank you." If Felicity lived up to that faith, she'd count herself successful.

Felicity's hand lightly skimmed the edge of a heavy wooden table as they passed through the corridor, feeling the grooves and intricacies of its carved surface. A delicately adorned music box on the surface caught her eye.

Curiosity got the better of her, and she lifted the lid. A soft melody, delicate and haunting, filled the space. The tune was vaguely familiar, like a lullaby from long ago.

"Ah," Mrs. Bennet remarked, stopping several steps ahead and turning about. "That belonged to Mrs. Deerwood. She left it behind on purpose, you know. Though they took many of their things with them, she said this music belonged in the house. She said it played the song of her heart."

Felicity closed her eyes for a moment, letting the music wash over her. "It's beautiful. It sounds the way I would expect memories to sound, or dreams . . . and perhaps a touch of sadness?"

Mrs. Bennet nodded. "Life here was not always easy for the former mistress of the house, at least at first. She came to this place as a new bride, much like you." Mrs. Bennet stared fondly at the music box, then sighed. "It was here she learned she would never have children of her own. But she had a way of turning sorrow into strength. This house, the village, they were her anchors. And more children roamed these halls, playing games and being doted on, than any other house in the county."

They walked on in companionable silence for a while. Something drew Felicity to the older woman, a sense of depth, or of experience and wisdom.

"Mrs. Bennet," she began hesitantly, "I hope it isn't too forward of me, but I feel a bit adrift here. My union with Mr. Harcourt was arranged swiftly, and I yearn for—well. For *more*. If my grandmother was still here, I would turn to her for guidance."

The housekeeper's expression turned sympathetic. "A woman's place is difficult, and all the more so when she hasn't anyone to guide her. I am sorry for that, Lady Felicity. Trust that anything you say to me I will hold in confidence. If there is anything I can do—"

The new bride didn't hesitate to ask. "Do you have any advice for me? For growing closer to my husband?"

Mrs. Bennet looked thoughtfully at Felicity, her eyes assessing yet kind. "Young love is like a budding flower," she began. "You cannot force it to bloom. It takes patience, nurturing, and understanding. And sometimes, it is the shared experiences, the trials, and joys that bring two souls closer."

Felicity hung onto every word, grateful for the guidance. Even if it sounded as though she required time more than anything. She could be patient, surely. How silly of her to think there were short-cuts. "Thank you, Mrs. Bennet. I will remember that."

The housekeeper placed a comforting hand on Felicity's arm. "You have a good heart, my lady. Let it guide you, and all will be well."

They continued the tour, and Felicity tucked away her worries. Time would bring her closer to her husband. That was all she needed. More time.

THE GOLDEN RAYS OF LATE MORNING SUNLIGHT SPILLED into Tad's study, making the polished wood of the desk glow. Quite a contrast to the dark ink in the open ledger in front of him. Neatly penned figures and numbers sprawled across the paper, but for Tad, they held little meaning at that moment. Instead, his quill, forgotten, dripped ink onto a blotter.

His thoughts were elsewhere—or rather, on someone else.

Lady Felicity.

Their wedding and journey to Winterway House felt like a dream, and he had yet to truly come to know his bride. He felt the distance between them, not just physically in the vastness of the house, but emotionally. He wanted to close it, but how?

The door to the study opened, and she entered, as if summoned by his thoughts. Felicity looked radiant, her face alight with enthusiasm. Her gown, a soft shade of lavender, accentuated her features, and for a moment, the world stopped. Each time he laid eyes on her, it struck him afresh just how enchanting she was. The sight of her in the room, the way the sunlight caught the gentle waves of her hair, took his breath away.

"Good morning, Mr. Harcourt," she said, the softness in her tone matching the warmth in her smile.

He rose, a bit too hastily, knocking the quill to the floor. "Good morning, Lady Felicity."

She came fully into the room, her hands tucked behind her back. "You need not be so formal when we are alone. As we are married, you may call me Felicity."

He swallowed. "Then you must stop with the *Mr. Harcourt* nonsense and call me Theodore." Then he winced. "Though I'll admit I might not know you're addressing me. No one has ever actually called me that. Except my father, on occasion."

She tilted her head with curiosity. "What do you wish to be called, then?"

"Tad," he blurted. "My family calls me Tad."

"Tad," she began again, using his name so familiarly it made his heart skip, "I've had some thoughts about the house and the village that I wanted to share."

He gestured for her to sit, but she seemed to prefer standing, excitement evident in her eyes as she came to stand at the edge of his desk.

"I came across a painting," she continued, "and from Mrs. Bennet, I learned of Mrs. Deerwood's wonderful traditions here. I thought we could continue them. Perhaps even host the winter ball and the New Year's Day celebrations she was so fond of."

Listening to her, Tad felt an odd mixture of emotions. There was admiration for Felicity's desire to immerse herself in the community, coupled with a surge of relief. Here was a direction, a purpose he could latch onto. She described her vision for their ballroom, turning it into a winter wonderland. Inviting everyone they could, including nobility, gentry, and merchants. Then visiting their tenants on Boxing Day, after Christmas. She spun her ideas so quickly, pacing as she spoke.

Her words painted a vivid picture in Tad's mind. One where they stood side by side, leading the community together, filling their house with joy, laughter, and warmth. When she paused for breath, she looked at him with an expectant tilt to her head, her hands held clasped together in front of her. "What do you think?"

"I must admit, I'm unfamiliar with many of the local customs and their expectations," he confessed, "but the idea of being more involved in the village appeals to me. I don't wish to be perceived as yet another an idle gentleman."

Felicity smiled, her gaze warm. "We can begin by immersing

ourselves in our new neighborhood. Perhaps we could take a walk in the village this afternoon? Meeting some of the merchants and shopkeepers? We ought to begin at once to familiarize ourselves with the town and its needs, ought we not?"

The suggestion was enticing. An opportunity to spend time with Felicity and understand their new home better, accomplishing both purposes in a single afternoon.

"I'd like that," he replied, his voice softer than he intended, grateful for the direction she provided. "Today isn't too soon for you? If you need more time to rest—"

"I am quite rested. I would very much like to go today. That is, if you are all right with the notion?"

"I think it an excellent idea. What time would you like to go?" He looked down at his desk and winced at the ledger. "I may need a little time. Would half past one o'clock be acceptable?"

"That would be perfect." The expression she bestowed upon him, the enthusiasm in her eyes, made him feel as though he'd received a beautiful gift. One he wasn't quite sure he deserved.

As she left the room, her joy surrounding him like a soft perfume, Tad felt an unfamiliar flutter in his chest. The daunting figures in the ledger no longer held his attention; the promise of the afternoon ahead had fully captured his mind.

Four

The grand wooden door of Winterway House opened without so much as a squeak, and Mr. Jones showed the new master and mistress of the house outside. Tad took in the view with a sense of pride. His hard work and his father's had brought him here, to this beautiful place far from London's crowds and air polluted by the smells of too many people in one place.

Here, the scent of trees and earth permeated everything. The world seemed to sparkle, despite the overcast sky. The vast grounds were a rich tapestry of faded browns and golds, with trees that had mostly shed their autumn splendor, standing tall and dark against the horizon. Though it wasn't winter by the calendar's reckoning, the air held that unmistakable briskness that hinted of the frosty season to come.

An open carriage awaited them, its glossy black frame contrasting with the beige upholstered seats. A pair of well-groomed horses stamped impatiently, their warm breaths creating ghostly puffs in the cold. The groom tipped his hat, ready to assist.

Felicity hesitated at the top of the steps, taking in the scenery with a deep, appreciative breath. Her cheeks took on a rosy hue from the chilly wind, and Tad, almost instinctively, moved closer, offering her his arm. She took it with a small, grateful smile.

As they descended the steps side by side, Tad couldn't help but admire how she looked with the backdrop of Winterway House. The muted colors of late autumn enhanced her radiant beauty, making her stand out like the last resilient bloom of the season.

The wind picked up slightly, tousling his hair and playing with Felicity's loose curls. They reached the carriage, and he helped her in, ensuring she was comfortable before taking his place with the leads.

He slapped the horse with the leathers, and the animal snorted as he began his trot down the lane.

As the carriage rolled toward the village, the rhythmic sounds of the horse's hooves and the creak of the wheels created a comforting cadence. The world outside was in a transitional phase, caught between the warm embrace of autumn and the chilly grasp of winter.

Tad breathed in deeply, appreciating the freshness that only the countryside could offer. "There's something invigorating about this air," he remarked, glancing over at Felicity. "I feel it recharges the senses. Do you feel it too?"

She smiled, eyes brightening. "Absolutely. The London air is so stifling in comparison. The country brings clarity, doesn't it? As if every breath has a touch of magic, reminding us we need to draw it in deeply to truly live."

Her fanciful way of speaking was rather endearing. He couldn't match it. But he wanted to try. "It always amazes me how the change of seasons can so profoundly affect one's mood.

Autumn feels like a celebration of life's richness with the harvest, while winter has always seemed bare and solemn."

Felicity tilted her head in thought. "I always felt that every season speaks to a different part of our soul. Autumn is a reflective time, allowing us to appreciate what we have. Winter, on the other hand, is introspective. It's nature's way of telling us to rest, seek warmth, and find comfort in our own company."

Tad's lips quirked up in a thoughtful smile. He wasn't a match for her. Perhaps it was all the poetry she read. "I've never thought of it that way. But now that you mention it, winter does make me gravitate towards the hearth, sharing stories or simply enjoying the warmth. It feels . . . intimate."

She returned his smile. "Perhaps it's nature's way of ensuring we stay close, forming bonds with the people in our home, and cherishing those around us when the world outside is cold and dark."

The comment seemed deeper than the subject of seasons, and Tad felt a pang of hope. Was she anticipating their winter to follow such a plan?

"It sounds as though you are looking forward to a winter away from London."

"I am." Felicity's eyes met his, and for a fleeting moment, the entire world reduced to just the two of them. "Because it will be my first with you, Tad," she whispered, her voice barely audible above the sounds of the carriage, yet perfectly clear to his eager ears.

The journey continued, and the vast fields slowly transitioned to structured lanes, bordered by hedgerows and the occasional cottage. As they neared Lynford Hollow, Tad felt a genuine appreciation for the village that had so swiftly welcomed him.

Whitewashed buildings, some timber-framed and others

constructed of brick, lined the central lane. Each one was unique, standing as a testament to various eras of architecture, but all bore that undeniable English charm. From the chimneys, delicate tendrils of smoke ascended, promising warm hearths within, and the merry laughter of children playing on cobbled streets resonated through the air.

As they navigated the lanes, Tad pointed out the landmarks he had come to know since purchasing Winterway House a month prior. "That's the blacksmith's forge," he gestured to a building where the rhythmic clang of metal could be heard. "And just there is Mrs. Tillman's bakery. I've been told she makes the most delightful scones, though I've yet to have the pleasure."

Felicity's gaze darted keenly about, absorbing every detail. "The village has such a vibrancy to it," she noted, her voice laced with curiosity.

"It certainly does," Tad replied with a nod. "I've only scratched the surface of Lynford Hollow's offerings, but what I've seen has been truly charming. The people here are most welcoming."

Many of the villagers gave a nod or a wave as the carriage passed. Although they were still becoming acquainted with Tad, their greetings were sincere. He reciprocated with warm smiles, ensuring Felicity felt connected to these early glimpses of village life.

Though his own familiarity with Lynford Hollow was still in a formative stage, Tad hoped the village would be a place they both could come to cherish. A place where, over time, they would lay down shared memories and build lasting connections.

The carriage rattled to a gentle stop outside The Hollow's Hearth, the local public house that stood as a welcoming beacon at the entrance of Lynford Hollow. Its wooden sign, painted with an image of a roaring fire, creaked as it swayed in the gentle breeze. The hum of conversation from the villagers inside filtered out, accompanied by the rich aroma of roasted meats and the tang of freshly tapped ale.

A young lad, no more than ten, with scruffy hair and pinked cheeks, dashed over from the side of the building. He eyed the carriage with wide-eyed admiration.

"Are you the Mr. Harcourt that bought up the Winterway house?" the boy asked.

Tad hadn't encountered this particular child before, but wasn't surprised people knew him on sight. "I am the very same," he said from his seat atop the carriage. "And this is Lady Felicity Harcourt, my wife."

It was the first time he'd introduced her as such. The words gave him a thrill he couldn't explain, making his heart swell with pride. *His wife.*

The remembrance he'd done nothing to merit that connection, however, immediately deflated him. Tad stole a glance at Felicity, searching her eyes for some hint of regret or uncertainty, but found none. Yet, the thought stayed, feeding his doubts from the evening before.

The war between hope and fear in his mind would soon exhaust him.

Did she see him as her equal, or was she merely playing the part expected of her? The question ate at him, casting a shadow over the day that had started so brightly.

"Need a hand with the horse, sir?" the child asked, a hopeful tone in his voice. It brought Tad somewhat out of the sudden onset of gloom.

"What's your name, lad?" He stepped down from the carriage to the cobbles.

"Jeremiah. My father owns the pub, sir."

"Well Jeremiah, are you good with horses?" He narrowed his eyes, scrutinizing the boy.

The child's chest puffed out. "I'm the best with them, Mr. Harcourt. I always tend to the guests' horses. Mules, too. They like me."

"Truly? How can you tell?"

"They don't shy away when I brush them. And their ears perk up when I speak to them. My papa says I have a way with them. That they can tell I'm a friend." The child's eyes sparkled with quiet pride.

"It sounds as though you're fit for the job."

A fierce nod accompanied Jeremiah's "yes, sir."

Tad pulled a coin from his pocket and handed it to the boy. "I'm sure my horse would prefer your company over wandering the village with us. Would you mind keeping an eye on him?" Tad offered the boy a smile. "We shan't be long."

The boy accepted the coin with a grin, his face lighting up. "Of course, sir! He'll be well looked after."

Tad turned to Felicity, trying not to notice the amusement in her eyes as he helped her from the carriage. "You have a way with children, it seems," she commented, nodding toward the beaming boy who was now proudly holding the horse's bridle.

Tad shrugged. There was no use taking any credit for the boy's glee. "They're the heart of places like this—full of energy and promise. I imagine he'd be as friendly to anyone else offering him coin, though."

Her smile faltered.

Why had he sounded so dismissive? His father said things like that. Implying money was the answer to everything. Tad hadn't wanted to make it sound that way.

He couldn't do anything right.

He extended his arm to her and tried for a lighter tone. "Shall we?"

She looped her arm through his, her touch sending a faint tingle up his arm. "Lead the way."

As they ventured deeper into the village, the couple passed the draper's shop, where bolts of colorful fabrics were displayed proudly in the window. Next to it was a haberdasher, its shelves lined with spools of thread, buttons, and ribbons. The soft chime of the apothecary's bell rang out as an elderly woman exited, a small paper-wrapped package clutched in her hand.

With each shop they passed, Tad tried to relay what he knew. "That's Mrs. Thatcher's drapery," he pointed out. "I ordered some of my linens there when I first arrived. And over there, Mr. Wentworth's provision shop. Best jams in Essex, or so I'm told."

Felicity laughed, the sound bright and easing his worry in a way that surprised him. "You seem to have acquainted yourself rather quickly."

He shot her a playful grin. "I had to. Especially if I was to impress a certain lady with my knowledge of local delicacies."

The door to Wentworth's shop opened quite suddenly, the jingle from the bell inside accompanying the man's jovial grin. "Mr. Harcourt, I knew 'twas you. And this must be your new missus."

Tad glanced at Felicity, and his wife raised her eyebrows at him as amusement sparked in her eyes.

He led her to the shop as he answered. "Indeed, Mr. Wentworth. Lady Felicity Harcourt, may I present to you Mr. Wentworth, as fine a shopkeeper as ever you could meet."

Mr. Wentworth bowed while Felicity inclined her head to him.

"It is a real pleasure, my lady. The whole town's been waiting to see the new mistress of the big house."

"Thank you, Mr. Wentworth. I hope I don't disappoint anyone's expectations." The lightness of her answer made Tad relax, until she peeked up at him from the corner of her eye. "Mr. Harcourt was just telling me you carry the best jams in Essex?"

Mr. Wentworth grinned. "Indeed. And he'd know best, my lady. He's tried every bit of my stock and sent the staff for several jars, too. You'll insult your cook, Mr. Harcourt, if you like our jams better'n hers."

Heat crept up the back of Tad's neck as he cleared his throat. "I will do my best not to earn her displeasure. Thank you, Mr. Wentworth."

The shopkeeper looked through the window into his shop, spying one of the customers he'd left inside at the counter. "I'd better pop back inside. A pleasure to meet you, my lady. Good day, Mr. Harcourt."

After he went back inside, the jingling bell muted by the closed door, Tad glanced down at Felicity to see her biting her lip, the corners of her mouth turned upward.

"It would seem you've tried the famous jams, then?"

He raised his shoulders in a sheepish shrug. "Every flavor available, I'm afraid."

"Oh, dear." The laughter didn't escape her lips, but he saw it in her eyes. And he wanted to tempt it all the way out.

He heaved a dramatic sigh. "Indeed. I'm afraid it's become a weakness. I visit Wentworth's every time I'm in the village. I go inside, telling myself he might have a thing I need. Pencils. A handkerchief. Something quite innocent. But I always leave with more jam."

Her laughter burst through, and she playfully pushed her shoulder against his. "You have a sweet tooth!"

He hung his head. "Alas. You've discovered my greatest

secret." He hadn't taken part in such a ridiculous conversation in —well. He couldn't remember when. But it felt right. Perfect, even, so long as his wife looked at him with such mirth in her eyes and her pink lips forming a pretty smile.

"I intend to use it to my advantage, too." Her nose wrinkled as she narrowed her eyes. "If ever you are reluctant to let me have my way, I will bribe you with all manner of jams."

He shuddered. "That you would use my weakness in such a way is villainous, my lady."

"Not at all." She tipped her chin upward. "Merely innovative." Then she winked at him, and Tad's heart tried to grow wings and take flight. He swallowed it down and had to look away to collect himself.

Yet the banter continued as they strolled, with Felicity teasing and Tad replying in kind. He introduced her to everyone they passed, and each time he used the words *my wife*, he experienced a rush of heady excitement. Yet he was also immediately brought low again by his own stern reminder that his marriage to such a lovely woman had been mere chance. A formality, to grant his family better standing and ease him into the role of a gentleman rather than a mere merchant's son.

Felicity seemed at ease, laughing at his anecdotes, appreciating the village's charm. But every smile, every glance she threw his way, was like a mirror reflecting his own inadequacies. The nagging doubt clawed at him, gnawing at the edges of his newfound happiness.

What if he was never enough for her? What if this village, the life he was offering, was all a poor substitute for what she could have had?

THE VIBRANCY OF LYNFORD HOLLOW WAS UNEXPECTED. After the serene landscape of Winterway House and the frantic pace of London, the village offered Felicity a delightful change of scenery. The bright facades of the shops, the hum of daily life—it was all so refreshingly ordinary.

Walking arm in arm with Tad, Felicity watched with amusement as he pointed out various landmarks, exaggerating their attributes with humorous enthusiasm. There was an eagerness to his voice, a pride in his newfound community. And her heart danced with hope each time he took evident pleasure in introducing her as "his wife."

But soon after his pleasure, a shadow would cross his face, a fleeting moment of doubt that vanished almost before she could notice it.

She wanted to hold on to the warmth in his eyes, the sincerity of his smiles, but she couldn't silence a small voice that whispered doubts in her ear. Their marriage had begun as a convenience; could it truly become something more? Or was she merely a means to an end for him, a necessary part of a grander scheme?

Would she ever understand this tension within him?

They had turned down a lane with fewer people, and her husband's eagerness seemed to dwindle with the foot traffic.

"You're awfully quiet of a sudden," Felicity observed, her tone laced with concern.

He forced a smile, though his eyes hinted at a vulnerability she wished she could understand. "I'm merely thinking about how wonderful this place is, and how much more wonderful it is with you here."

Her cheeks warmed at the unexpected compliment. She wanted to press, to delve deeper into his thoughts, but the opportunity was lost as a cheerful, masculine voice called out to them.

"Ah, Mr. Harcourt! Good to see you about on this fine afternoon, sir. And this must be your lovely bride."

Turning, Felicity found herself facing a man in his early thirties, wearing the garb of a vicar, with a vibrant and smiling woman at his side.

Tad swiftly came to attention. "Ah. Lady Felicity, allow me to introduce Reverend George Moore."

"A pleasure, Lady Felicity. Let me present my wife, Mrs. Eliza Moore, to you both." The vicar indicated his wife, who curtsied prettily.

Mrs. Moore stepped forward, her warm brown eyes studying Felicity with interest. "I was delighted when I heard Winterway House had been purchased by a young gentleman, but it doubled when we learned he had a bride to bring home. Welcome to Lynford Hollow, Lady Felicity"

A smile spread across Felicity's face. "Thank you, Mrs. Moore. It's a pleasure."

Mrs. Moore's eyes sparkled with enthusiasm. "Have you ever visited the village before? Perhaps attended the winter festivities in Lynford Hollow? I have only been here the last two years, coming as a new bride myself. They are quite the event."

Felicity's eyes widened in curiosity. "No, I haven't had the pleasure. Are they different from London's celebrations?"

Mrs. Moore gave an enthusiastic nod. "While we may lack the grandeur of London's affairs, there's an intimacy and charm to our village gatherings. Families come together, homes are thrown open, and there's an enchanting candlelight procession through the village square on Christmas Eve."

"That sounds delightful," Felicity remarked, quite taken with the idea. "In London, such events can sometimes feel impersonal. Here, it seems there's a true sense of community. Everyone has been so kind already."

Mrs. Moore smiled in agreement. "Precisely. And speaking of community, I hope you will join our Ladies Aid Society. We come together often to plan events and to organize help for those in need."

Felicity's interest fully took hold of that information. "I've always enjoyed charity work. In London, I was involved in a few organizations that helped the less fortunate, but I had to give them up the last two years to tend to my late-grandmother's needs. I would dearly love to begin such work again."

"Oh, that's wonderful to hear," the vicar's wife exclaimed, clearly delighted. "We have a reading school, as well as a sewing circle that makes clothing for children. Your experience would be invaluable."

"I would be more than happy to help in any way I can," Felicity replied earnestly.

"Delightful. Perhaps we may walk together for a bit?" Mrs. Moore looked up at her husband, who nodded his ascent. Then she gestured for Felicity to join her. The women walked side-by-side with the men following behind.

They continued their stroll along the road. Their conversation effortlessly flowed from one topic to the next. They discussed the beauty of the Essex countryside, and Mrs. Moore shared descriptions of her favorite spots.

Finding a possible friend so soon brough a measure of comfort to Felicity's heart. It had been too long since she had spent time among women of her own age and station.

Throughout their conversation, Tad seemed to relax, chatting with Reverend Moore about the village's needs. However, Felicity couldn't rid herself of the feeling that something still bothered him. She resolved to find a quiet moment to talk, to understand the source of his unease.

As Felicity and Mrs. Moore meandered down the village's

main thoroughfare, their path naturally led them to the entrance of St. James's Chapel. Felicity paused, her gaze ensnared by the tranquil beauty before her. The chapel, with its rustic grey stone walls and slate roof dotted with moss, looked as though it had grown from the land, seamlessly blending with the nature surrounding it.

The tall trees cradling the sacred building whispered tales of bygone eras, their bare branches rustling in soft applause to the countless sermons and hymns they had borne witness to. She could almost hear the echoes of the past, a harmonious blend of joyous celebrations and solemn remembrances.

The graveyard, with its well-tended paths and array of tombstones, told stories of its own. Each marker, whether grand or humble, spoke of lives intertwined with the village's history.

Beside her, Mrs. Moore watched Felicity's rapt attention with a knowing smile. "It's quite something, isn't it?" she murmured.

Felicity nodded, then spoke with her voice hushed in reverence. "It's as if the very walls and stones are imbued with the soul of the community. It's beautiful."

Mrs. Moore's eyes twinkled. "It is the heart of Lynford Hollow. And now, it's a part of your story too."

For a moment, the two women stood in silent communion, letting the weight of history wash over them. A gentle nudge in Felicity's heart made her whisper, "It will be wonderful to call this place home."

The hush of the chapel's surroundings remained, only to be broken by Mr. Moore's warm voice. "You know, we'd be absolutely delighted if you both would join us for dinner this Sunday evening. It would give us a chance to properly welcome you to Lynford Hollow."

Mrs. Moore nodded in agreement, her eyes bright with anticipation. "Yes, and I'd love to introduce you to some of our friends, Lady Felicity. There are many truly wonderful people for you to meet."

Tad watched Felicity, obviously waiting for her to respond to the invitation. "That sounds lovely. We'd be honored."

Tad nodded in agreement. "We appreciate the offer. We'll look forward to it."

The sky had deepened into dusky shades of purples and blues, with the last traces of sunlight dipping below the horizon. A lamplighter appeared as they spoke, long stick in hand. She nodded as she lit the tall streetlamp nearest them, then left it casting a soft glow over the cobblestone path.

They bid their new friends farewell, and Tad escorted her back to the carriage. He helped her into the seat after giving the boy, Jeremiah, another coin. With a gentle lurch, they began their journey back to Winterway House.

A crisp chill crept into the air. The dried leaves along the road rustled, whispering secrets to the wind, and the first stars of the evening began to twinkle, like silent guardians watching over the village.

A shiver ran down her spine, more from the exhilaration of the day than the cold. Before she could react, she felt Tad's arm drape around her shoulders, pulling her closer to him. The warmth of his body acted as a shield against the evening's chill, and she nestled comfortably into his embrace.

Throughout the ride, Felicity was bathed in a sense of hopeful anticipation, her heart buoyed by the promise of new friendships and the moments shared with Tad. He, on the other hand, remained contemplative, his thoughts unspoken. But his grip around her never wavered, determinedly keeping her warm in his silence.

Five

DECEMBER 3RD

F elicity awoke, the morning light filtering faintly through
the heavy drapery of her chamber. The elegant room,
with its delicate furniture and pretty trimmings, felt
empty. She turned on her side, her hand reaching out to the
other half of the bed. It was empty and untouched.

Not what she had expected as a new bride. And if Tad hadn't
been so gentle, so thoughtful, she'd perhaps be relieved. Instead,
confusion batted her thoughts about in her head, rather like a cat
with a mouse.

The events of the previous day came to her mind. The laughter, the shared glances, the warmth of the villagers, and the
comforting presence of Tad beside her as they returned home.
Yet as soon as they had stepped over the threshold of Winterway
House, he'd changed. Gone was the tentative smile, replaced by a
mask of courtesy and aloofness.

She had initially appreciated his respectful distance, inter-
preting it as a sign of his understanding that their marriage was
still new. That they were still near strangers. But as the hours

passed and the night grew cold, doubts and fears pricked at her heart.

Did he not find her desirable? Though no great beauty, Felicity had thought herself somewhat attractive. Had she, in her eager attempts to know him, somehow miss-stepped? Or worse, was there a hidden love in his past who already held his affection? Perhaps he hadn't wanted to marry her at all. She'd been chosen by his father and a solicitor.

She'd been desperate for a safe place to fall after mourning her grandmother's passing. Her future had been uncertain. Bleak. Tad, as a man of means with a supportive family, could have married anyone. Why hadn't he found a woman on his own?

These were all questions she ought to have asked before. Instead, she'd been relieved to find a rescue. And that had been enough.

She drew the blankets tightly around her, attempting to ward off the chill of uncertainty. "I must be patient, as Mrs. Bennet advised." she whispered into the quiet room. "It's only been a few days. We're still finding our rhythm, learning the steps of a new dance takes longer. And marriage . . ." She laughed at herself. "It must be the most intricate dance of all."

Before her thoughts could spiral further, the door to the corridor burst open, revealing a grinning Clara. Her cheeks were flushed from excitement, and her eyes sparkled with mischief.

"Lady Felicity," she exclaimed, barely containing her excitement, "You won't believe it! The world's turned into a winter fairyland." She came in with a breakfast tray, putting it aside in a rush. "You must see it at once."

Without waiting for a response, Clara dashed to the window, flinging open first the heavy curtains, then the window. A gust of cold wind blew in, carrying with it the soft flurries of snow. The grounds of the estate, the trees, the hedges, everything was blanketed in a pristine layer of white. The world outside seemed to shimmer, like a painting come alive.

Felicity's worries momentarily forgotten, she sat up, drawn to the beauty of the scene. The snow had a magical quality, turning the familiar landscape into something out of a fairy tale as the maid had said.

"Oh, Clara," Felicity breathed, her voice filled with wonder, "it's simply enchanting."

Clara, smiling broadly, nodded in agreement. "It's the village's first snow, my lady. Always special. Perhaps," she added with a cheeky wink, "it's a sign of good things to come."

Felicity rose from the bed and went to the window, letting herself be swept away by the moment. Yes, there were chilling uncertainties, but there was also beauty and hope. And she was determined to embrace it all.

Clara went to the hearth, stirring up the banked embers and adding wood and coal to the fire to build it up. "You will want to go out immediately after breakfast, as usual?"

Her maid knew her well. Felicity never hesitated to take a walk in newly fallen snow. "Yes."

As Felicity drew a shawl around her shoulders, settling in the chair to take her breakfast by the fire, her gaze inadvertently shifted to the painting hung over the room's mantel. It was the very painting she had discovered amidst the forgotten trinkets of the old, unused rooms of Winterway House. Mrs. Bennet had worked quickly to hang it up, it would seem.

Today, however, she peered at it more closely. The muted colors of the painting, the delicate brush strokes—it all depicted a winter scene. She could see a thin layer of snow covering rooftops, the pathways, and the trees of the depicted village. The overcast skies in the artwork seemed to mirror the skies outside her window.

How had she missed those details before?

She rose from the chair and stepped nearer. Her fingers lightly traced the snowy imagery, marveling at the intricacies of the village buildings. She recalled the note she'd found with the painting, a simple plea to "Please take care of our little village." At the time, she'd thought it a quaint sentiment. Now, with the snow outside and the scenery in the painting, it felt almost providential.

The soft clatter of dishes interrupted her musings, and she turned to find Clara preparing her morning chocolate the way Felicity liked it best.

"Here you are, my lady." She handed the cup to Felicity with a grin. "I'll set out your clothes while you eat. Oh." She blinked suddenly. "Do you wish for me to inform Mr. Harcourt of your intentions to go out? Perhaps he'd like to join you."

Felicity hesitated, biting her lower lip. "No, Clara. Let him be. I don't wish to impose upon his time or distract him from his own pursuits."

Clara nodded, and her eyes went soft with an understanding that made Felicity blush. "As you wish, my lady."

As Clara busied herself with gathering clothing suitable for a winter walk, Felicity took a last look at the painting. Whatever its story, it now held a place in her heart. With newfound determination, she decided to embrace the snow-covered day. Immediately after breakfast.

After her faithful maid bundled her against the cold weather, Felicity fairly skipped out of doors. Likely, there were duties for her to see to as the new mistress of Winterway. But those could wait.

She opened the music box when she passed it in the corridor, giving a satisfied nod of her head when the music drifted into the silence. On a day full of promise, the gentle melody ought to remind her what it meant to have a song in her heart.

When Felicity had moved from schoolroom to Society functions, she'd scoffed at what she deemed her previous behavior as childish. It was on a morning like this, with snow falling softly outside the window. Her grandmother had suggested they both go outside to catch snowflakes on their tongues.

"How silly," Felicity had said with a wrinkle of her nose, though she dearly wished to go outside to feel the cold on her cheeks. "I'm too grown for that now, Grandmama."

Her grandmother had given her a patient look. "Remember, my dear, life is a series of fleeting moments. When you find a spark of joy, even if it's as delicate as a snowflake or a butterfly's wing, embrace it. It is in those brief moments that we truly live."

Still acting as though she was too mature for such things, Felicity had gone out that day, and she'd learned the truth of her grandmother's words in the years since.

Frosted gardens always bore a certain magic for Felicity. She stepped outside, the world hushed by the snow's embrace. Her footfalls made soft crunching sounds on the snow-covered gravel path, the stillness amplifying every sound.

Venturing deeper into the gardens, a delicate iron gate came into view, its spires capped with snow. Just past the gate was a secluded rose garden. Bare thorny branches crisscrossed like delicate lacework against the white backdrop. The blooms had retreated from winter's grasp, but their trembling thorns bore a promise of a return in the spring.

Past the rose garden, the silhouette of a stone fountain loomed, icicles dripping from the top layer where water had spilled freely the day before. Surrounding it, little birds hopped about, their tiny beaks pecking through the snow in search of food.

A pang of sympathy struck her heart, and she said quietly, "I must bring breadcrumbs next time."

Any scraps the kitchen could spare, she'd scatter about for the animals whose food sources would turn scarce as the season turned.

The soft snowfall continued, and a flake landed on the tip of her nose. Making her giggle like a child.

On an impulse, Felicity tilted her head back, eyes closed, tongue outstretched. She could feel the cold, delicate touch of snowflakes melting on her tongue, taking her back to the time when she'd had her grandmother to look after her.

A giddy joy bubbled up, and she spread her arms wide, giving in to the whimsy in her heart. She spun in a circle, feeling the world blur around her, the cold air rushing past her cheeks. The weight of her winter skirts flared out as she turned, creating patterns on the snow beneath.

Her twirling joy was interrupted by a sudden awareness. A prickling sensation of being watched. Her spins slowed, and she came to an abrupt stop, her skirts settling heavily around her.

Before her stood Tad, his tall frame imposing. He was merely a silhouette against the white landscape, standing still behind the iron gate, his gaze firmly on her. There was no mistaking it. He had seen her moment of abandon.

For a heartbeat, in the stillness, doubt flickered in her mind. Her cheeks flushed, not just from the cold but from the realization she'd been caught in an unguarded moment.

Would he censure her for the childish behavior?

Her breaths came out as visible puffs in the cold air, and she hesitated to greet him, uncertain of what to say or do next.

THE SNOW HAD ALWAYS HELD A UNIQUE ALLURE FOR TAD. As a child, he'd watched it blanket the docks from the windows of their family's rooms above his father's offices, but he'd never been allowed the luxury of losing himself in its magic. Work, duty, and responsibility had been drilled into him from a young age, and somewhere along the way, he'd forgotten the innocent pleasure of simply being in the moment.

Even when his father had earned enough to lease a town-house, Tad hadn't been given time to enjoy his youth. Instead, there had been tutors. A dozen of them, at least, tasked with catching him up to the level of education boys with aristocratic backgrounds had already achieved. Then his father sent him to Oxford, and from there Tad had been brought back into the family business.

He knew nothing but ledgers, numbers, hard work, and toil. Snow slowed deliveries and soon turned black with grime. The cold slowed the dockworkers. The threat of illness, of storms, and delays, came with the cold. Along with a myriad of other things that could harm a merchant's business.

And he didn't know how else to think of it, but seeing the beautiful white landscape that morning, rather than feel the dread his father expressed on such occasions, Tad's heart lifted with unexpected enjoyment.

It was beautiful.

Standing by his study window, Tad's attention had been drawn to the moving figure below. His wife had left the house for the world of white. Dressed in a dark green gown with a red hooded cloak, she made a vibrant silhouette against the pristine snow.

Felicity made her way into the gardens. For a moment, he hesitated. Then, compelled by a silent force, he hurried from the room, shouting for his coat and hat. Gloves.

He needed to join her.

It wasn't just a husband's concern for his wife's well-being; there was something else—a pull, a charm that she seemed to emanate. Drawing him to her.

Of course, he had to be practical, too. She could catch cold. Slip on ice and fall, all alone. It was best he was there, to look after her.

Wasn't that a husband's duty, to look after his wife?

Yet he hesitated the moment he stepped outside. He'd rushed through the house, had prepared himself to run through the gardens to catch up to her. Surely, he'd seem overeager. Perhaps she'd think him odd or pathetic. And he couldn't bear that.

So he took his time, weaving his way through the garden, following her footprints that slowly filled in with more snow.

From a distance, he watched her wander, noting how she moved with a grace that seemed sophisticated even as her delight of the snow was unrestrained. The way she interacted with the garden, her gentleness with the birds, the soft promise to bring them food next time—she was enchanting.

Her joyous spin amidst the snowflakes truly captivated him. The sight stirred something deep within. A feeling he hadn't recognized for the longest time: longing. A longing to shed the weights and worries that shackled him, to join her in that innocent merriment, to feel the snowflakes on his own skin and taste them on his lips.

As she spun, the world around her seemed to blur into an array of whites and grays, her red and green figure remaining the only distinct thing in his vision. He'd seen her formal, he'd seen her in quiet contemplation, but this...this was a Felicity he had not known—a side that beckoned him closer.

When she stopped, her gaze finding his, time seemed to stretch endlessly. There was surprise in her eyes, a hint of vulnerability, perhaps even embarrassment. He wished he could convey the warmth, the profound admiration he felt, the desire to join her in that dance. Words failed him.

His life followed a structured cadence—every moment, every action calculated, measured. And here she was, presenting a melody he wasn't sure he knew how to dance to.

But oh, how he wanted to learn.

Taking a deep breath, he tried to find words, any words, that would break the silence between them. He walked towards her, each step an attempt to close the distance—not just physical, but whatever distance existed in their understanding of one another. The snow crunched underfoot, until he came to a stop directly in front of her.

"Good morning, Tad," she whispered. She immediately bit her bottom lip, chewing on it as uncertainty filled her eyes. He found her adorable, and immediately realized he'd never thought such a thing about another person in his life.

Tad's heart beat quickened.

"Good morning, Felicity," he replied, his own voice betraying him with a slight waver. His eyes dropped to her lips, then quickly away, as if caught in some minor transgression. "I saw you from the window."

"I hope you do not mind, that I came out..." Her words trailed away as he started shaking his head.

"No. Of course not. These are your gardens. You don't need anyone's permission to enjoy them." He cleared his throat. "They are quite a different place than when I last saw them."

Her gloved hand gestured delicately to the snowfall and the distant trees. "It's magical, don't you think?" she asked softly, looking at him. "It's as if the world has dressed itself in its finest especially for us."

Tad's breath caught at her words, and he found himself moving closer, drawn to her as if by a magnet. He could see the flush on her cheeks from the cold, the sparkle in her eyes that wasn't solely a reflection of the snow.

"I believe," he said, his voice dropping lower, "that you bring the magic, Felicity. The world might dress itself, but you—" He paused, searching for the right words, words that would say what he was beginning to feel. "You make it come alive."

Her breath hitched, and she looked down, a smile playing on her lips as if she were trying to hide it. Then her eyes met his, and in them he saw something that made his heart leap.

Understanding. Connection.

"Would you like to walk with me, Tad?" she asked, her voice soft, inviting. Her eyes sparkled with a playful challenge. "There's a part of the garden, over by the old oak, where the snowfall looks absolutely enchanting."

He studied her, surprised by the invitation but intrigued. A walk through the snowy garden, only the two of them, felt like a chance to break away from the constraints he'd placed upon himself. If Felicity invited him, he wasn't forcing his company upon her. Giving him a chance to know her better.

"I would be delighted to accompany you, my dear," he replied, offering his arm. The formality of the gesture coupled with the endearment linked the world he knew and this new, unexplored territory with her.

Her hand slipped into the crook of his arm, and they set off for the oak, their footprints marking a new path in the fresh snow.

"It's been ages since I've taken a walk in the snow," Felicity remarked, her eyes fixed on the snowflakes dancing in the air. "It feels like a fairy-tale, doesn't it?"

"It does," Tad agreed, watching her face light up as she spoke. "Though I must confess, I haven't allowed myself to enjoy such simple pleasures in years."

Felicity's glance held a measure of surprise. "Whyever not?"

"Work, duty, responsibility," he replied, his voice tinged with regret. "It's all I've known for so long."

"Surely, you must have things other than work to think on. Some dreams yet to accomplish," she prodded gently, looking into his eyes, encouraging him. "Things you look forward to enjoying outside of your duty."

He hesitated, but the sincerity in her tone gave him confidence to answer. "I once wanted to travel," he admitted, his voice soft. "To see the world beyond England's shores. To go where my family's cargo makes port, across the Channel at the very least. There was always too much to do."

She squeezed his arm affectionately, her touch warm even through the layers of fabric. "It's never too late to dream, Tad."

"And you, Felicity?" he asked, curious. "What dreams fill your heart?"

Her smile appeared, slight and thoughtful, a faraway look in her eyes. "I'm not certain. My grandmother's care consumed me for the last several years. And then losing her, all those months ago …" She shivered. "I was so alone. The only person left who cared for me was gone. I missed her—I still miss her—terribly. I haven't had much chance to dream. I have been far too occupied with the difficult realities of my life."

He was a cad. A brute. He hadn't spoken to her of her grandmother even once. And he knew she had lost the woman who raised her, but somehow he hadn't realized how alone she'd been. Here he sulked about his inability to work in the offices where he'd grown from child to man, and she had lost everything.

Why had he let his father make this arrangement? Why had he gone along with it? The poor woman, leaping into marriage with a stranger as a way of dealing with the *difficult realities* of her life.

He swallowed back the bitter taste the thought left on his tongue.

Felicity, oblivious to his inner debasement, mused aloud. "I used to love to create, to paint. Now, I think my greatest desire is to live a life filled with meaning. I want to bring cheer and warmth into the lives of others."

He had married an angel. That's all there was to it.

When they reached the old oak, they found it covered in a delicate layer of frost and snow, branches reaching out like arms in a graceful pose. The scene was breathtaking, and they stood together in silence, taking it in.

Felicity's hand found a snow-laden branch, and she gently shook it, causing a flurry of snowflakes to fall around them. She looked up at Tad, her eyes wide and bright, full of wonder and joy.

He met her gaze, feeling a connection that went beyond mere attraction. In that moment, he realized that he was not merely looking at a beautiful woman in a beautiful setting. He was looking at someone who saw the world in a way he had forgotten, someone who could teach him to see it that way again.

"Thank you for sharing this with me," he whispered, his voice filled with soft gratitude.

Her eyes softened. "I'm glad you joined me on my walk."

And as they continued their way, Tad knew that he had taken

a step closer to something profound, something that he had not even known he was missing. In the quiet wonder of the snowy garden, he had found not only a connection with Felicity but a new understanding of himself.

He still had dreams to dream.

Six

W hen they reentered the house, Felicity's cheer was quite restored. But her nose felt nearly frostbitten and her fingers numb. She looked down at the hem of her dress and sighed. "I am soaked through and half frozen."

In the midst of taking off his gloves, Tad started. "That will not do." He glanced at the footman who had taken her cloak. "See to it that tea and a warm blanket are brought to my study at once, for Lady Felicity."

"Yes, Mr. Harcourt." The servant bowed, then scurried off to do Tad's bidding.

She shivered and put her arms around herself. "I have no wish to disturb you. I can warm up in my room."

"The study is exceptionally warm." His dark eyes studied her features in such concern that her heart thrummed happily beneath the inspection. "And as I am to blame for keeping you out in the cold so long, I must be the one to put things to rights." His smile, though small, held a hint of teasing she found rather sweet.

"Very well. If you insist."

"I do. What sort of husband would I be if I didn't look after my wife?" He held out his arm as he had in the garden, and she took it with a smile. How long before such a thing was a habit between them? "We cannot have you catching a chill."

She let him lead her up the stairs and down the corridor to his study, a room that she had loved the first time she'd seen it the day before. The walls were dark green, reminding her of the depths of a fairy tale forest, with bookshelves on either side of a large hearth. His desk was positioned so he could both see anyone who entered the room and turn easily to look out the window. Which was how he had spotted her in the garden.

He led her to the small couch, sized to comfortably fit two, in front of the fire. As she settled on the cushion, he stoked the flames and added coal to the blaze. "There. We will have you warmed through in no time."

"Thank you. You must be cold too." She stretched her feet toward the fire, and his gaze landed on her half-boots and damp hem.

"You are my first concern, my dear."

The affectionate term had surprised her when he used it outside, and when her husband dropped to his knees on the rug in front of her, Felicity couldn't stop a small gasp.

"Let me help you with these. You'll warm faster without damp boots." He glanced up, already holding the heel of her boot in one large hand. His eyes went wide. "If that is all right with you. That is, if you do not mind—"

"If *you* do not mind playing lady's maid," she said quickly, not hiding her amusement. "I will gladly accept your assistance."

Twin red spots appeared on his cheeks, and when he lowered his head to concentrate on her bootlaces, she saw the tips of his ears had turned red as well. She never felt his touch on her stockinged foot or ankle, for it was quite gingerly and only on her boots. Then he pivoted where he knelt and stood them up by the fire.

"You ought to remove your own," she pointed out.

"Yes. Of course." He sat on the edge of the sofa next to her, crossing his leg and deftly removing his own footwear. He placed his boots next to hers, then knelt to tend to the fire. They were taller and larger, and the contrast of the narrow heels of her boots next to the thick soles of his made her smile.

"I've never really looked at men's boots before," she admitted when he caught her staring. She shrugged helplessly at his furrowed brow. "The dowager house where my grandmother raised me didn't see many gentleman visitors."

"What of that fellow from the wedding?" her husband asked from where he crouched near the hearth. "Lord Something-or-Other."

It took her a moment to remember, and then she had to grin. "Lord William Thursby. His grandmother was a close friend to my own. They were both presented at court the same year, sharing nearly a lifetime of friendship together. I met him a handful of times when our grandmothers would visit with one another."

The first time they met, her grandmother had ventured to visit her old friend at the Thursby home and invited Felicity along. When she met Lord William she immediately discovered him to be an incurable flirt. She knew at once he meant nothing by his words and sly smiles, and she'd chosen amusement rather than annoyance when in his presence every time their grandmothers came together. The last time she saw him, the time before the wedding, the circumstances were quite changed.

"His grandmother passed two years ago," she remembered aloud. "He came to tell my grandmother in person." She looked down at her hands, reflecting on that day with a shake of her head.

Her grandmother had been heartbroken at the news. Lord William had stayed on for dinner to share memories of his grandmother, then left. He'd sent Felicity his condolences when he learned of her grandmother's passing. A brief, impersonal note. They hadn't been friends, exactly. But they had both loved the elderly women who raised them.

"I certainly didn't expect to see him at our wedding. I'm hardly acquainted with him."

"Was he not among your suitors?"

Felicity shook her head. "No. But then, I don't suppose I had very many suitors."

"I find that difficult to believe." Though his eyes had widened somewhat, his gentle smile made her wonder if he was only feigning surprise.

"I wasn't exactly well-connected, growing up the orphaned granddaughter of a widowed countess. We lived in a dower house not more than two miles from London. Yet I didn't have a large enough dowry to tempt anyone to come near." She gave a helpless shrug. "I was quite content not to wed young, and later it felt like I would be abandoning my grandmother, which wouldn't be fair considering all she did to raise me. Marriage was an afterthought, until she grew ill, and then it was simply too late."

Too late to be presented. Too late to court. With an ill grandmother her only family, there was no one to find her a match or chaperone her to events where men could gawk at her and estimate if her dowry made her worth the trouble of courtship and marriage, with a grandmother in tow.

"I can understand contentment and the fear of leaving your grandmother behind. It sounds to me as though the gentlemen who were aware of you were foolish, selfish creatures. Anyone who met you would know you at once for the treasure you are."

Her cheeks heated. "Tad. What a thing to say."

"I stand by it. And I am suddenly quite grateful London bachelors are fools," he said in an offhand sort of way. "Had you many men calling on you, I doubt I would now hold the place of husband."

Her lips parted in surprise, but she didn't have the chance to respond to such a bold statement.

A soft knock on the door preceded the arrival of their tea, along with cake thoughtfully provided by the cook. Clara followed behind the footman who carried the tea tray, her own hands full of a blanket and Felicity's house slippers.

The maid's eyebrows rose as she came around the furniture to find Felicity already without boots. She slipped the satin, wool-lined shoes onto her mistress's feet, tucked the blanket around her, then withdrew with a rather smug tilt to her lips.

Felicity started to rise to prepare the tea, but her husband already undertook the duty. She settled back into the comfortable corner of the couch.

"Lemon or honey?" he asked, eyebrows drawn together as he poured from the pot into two cups.

"Honey, please."

"Milk?"

"No, thank you."

No man had ever prepared a cup of tea for her before. Nor brought it to her with such an expression of concentration on his face as Tad did. He returned a moment later with a slice of cake on a plate, then saw to himself before settling on the furniture beside her again. He glanced up at her, and one corner of his mouth hitched upward.

"Perhaps your maid would have seen to your needs better than I have."

She shook her head and sipped at her tea, closing her eyes to savor the sweet taste of honey and something more. Ginger, given the added warmth of the spice. They said nothing while they sipped at the tea and nibbled at the cake, and the room grew warmer.

Tad sat quite stiffly beside her, and when she studied him she caught sight of the damp wool on the back of his coat. Snow must've fallen between his thick, outer coat and the one he wore now.

"I worry that you will be the one to catch a chill," she said, and his cup stilled midway between plate and his lips. She pointed to the edge of his coat. "That wool is quite damp, Tad. You should remove your coat."

His ears pinked again. "You would not mind?"

"It is only the two of us here, and we are man and wife. I will not be offended if you go about our home, indeed in your own study, in your shirtsleeves and waistcoat." It was only practical, really.

He put his tea and plate down on the table beside the sofa, then stood and tugged his coat off with his back to her. When it slid off his shoulders, she raised her eyebrows with interest. He was as broad-shouldered in the single layer of linen shirt as he'd been with the coat, though she realized his waist was more tapered than she had thought.

Her husband cut a fine figure. Her cheeks warmed as he settled again beside her, silently taking up his tea. Neither of them spoke as they finished their refreshment, and even after she had passed him her empty cup and dish, she said nothing. Instead, she pulled the blanket up to her chin and sank back into the soft velvet cushion of the sofa.

Tad shifted, looking from her to the fire, then he rose abruptly and went to the shelves. He selected a book and smiled at her as he returned. "Our friend Donne is still in the drawing room. But I found this among the books here. It seems Mr. Deerwood enjoyed poetry." He held the slim volume out to her.

Poems, in Two Volumes, by William Wordsworth. She accepted the book.

"Did he leave behind his library with the estate?" she asked with interest, turning the pages of Volume I. "I doubt I could ever part with a favorite book. I packed a crate full of my favorites, you know, though they have not yet arrived."

"I didn't know." He sat beside her, his arm along the back of the furniture as he leaned close to turn the page of the book in her hand. "And yes, Mr. Deerwood left much in the house. Furnishings, artwork. That was part of the reason I chose this estate above the other options. Though you are welcome to change anything you like, I thought the prospect of filling an empty home might be too daunting a task in the beginning. For both of us."

Even though they hadn't met until the day before the wedding, he'd thought of her. Considered her place in his life, in his home, in such a way as to plan for her coming. That reminder brought a warmth to her heart, and a quiet, soft longing. She leaned a little more against the arm he'd draped along the back of the sofa, lowering her eyes to the first page.

She read the title of the poem aloud. "*To the Daisy*."

TAD LISTENED AS FELICITY SPOKE THE WORDS OF THE poem with a gentle cadence, and her voice floated through the air as she read aloud. The delicate lilt of her words stirred something within him, a warmth that reached beyond the mere heat of the fire. He found himself drawn to the curve of her lips as she pronounced each word, and the dainty way her fingers held the pages.

In the days that had led up to their marriage, he'd been lost in a whirl of confusion, anticipation, and a curious kind of longing. Now, as he sat beside her, the soft curve of her body an arm's length away, the reality of their union settled within him.

She was his wife. His partner. Someone he had vowed to protect and cherish. Yet, they were still strangers, their lives and emotions tangled together in a way neither had quite prepared for. Her nearness was both exhilarating and terrifying, filled with a promise he didn't yet know how to fulfill.

As she continued to read, her voice filled with an eagerness for the words, he found his eyes wandering over her face. The late morning light from the window bathed her features in its glow, highlighting the graceful line of her neck, the slope of her shoulder, and the golden curl that had escaped the most intricate twists of her hair.

He couldn't help but marvel at her loveliness. The grace and intelligence that lay behind her sparkling eyes. Her curiosity, her kindness, her way of looking at the world; all of it drew him in, making him ache with a desire to know her more deeply.

And yet, the intensity of those feelings held him back. He was her husband, yes, but he was also a gentleman, bound by the codes of conduct that defined his new world. A world he didn't yet understand, or truly belong to. He wanted to be close to her, to cross the boundary that propriety and unfamiliarity had placed between them. Yet he feared to overstep, to presume too much too soon.

As she reached the end of the poem, her eyes met his, and

something unspoken passed between them. A connection, tentative and fragile, that sent a thrill down his spine.

"That was beautiful," he said, his voice husky with emotion. "I've never heard Wordsworth read with such feeling."

She blushed, looking down at the book in her lap. "I've always loved poetry," she said, her voice soft. "It makes you consider the commonplace more deeply, wholeheartedly."

"Yes," he agreed, feeling the truth of her words resonate within him. "It certainly does."

He wanted to reach out, to touch her hand, to let her know without words how deeply he was affected by her presence. But what if he frightened her with the intensity of his feelings?

A woman unfamiliar with men couldn't possibly understand what he felt. What if his desires caused her disgust? How were gentlemen supposed to show their noble-born wives how they felt?

Instead, he turned to look at the fire, his mind a turmoil of conflicting thoughts. He'd taken the first tentative steps on a journey that would challenge him in ways he had never anticipated.

Their relationship was still new, a bloom waiting to unfold. But as he glanced at her once more, her eyes still fixed on the pages of the book, he knew with a deep, unshakeable certainty that he was ready to discover all that lay ahead.

How would he find out if she was ready too?

She idly turned a few pages in the book, smiling to herself, then raised her gaze to his with a gleam of amusement in her eyes. But that amusement faded when her hazel eyes met his, and he saw the copper flecks amid the brown and green of her iris. Like new pennies, waiting for him to gather them up. To count each one. To treasure them.

He bent closer to her. They were so near. Time slowed as he

studied her and let her study him, the moment drawn-out until his heart felt near to breaking. Her breath mingled with his, warm and scented with spice and cake. Tad leaned in, focused on the bow of her pink lips. Wondering if they would feel petal-soft against his. He had every intention of finding out, right that moment.

He'd never kissed a woman before. He'd been too busy, working too hard, to give much thought to the daughters of other merchants. And now he had a wife, a woman of noble birth. A *lady*.

What if she didn't wish to be kissed? What if she thought she had no choice in the matter?

Her lips parted. Her lashes lowered. And she leaned forward. Coming toward him, rather than remaining stiff or pulling back.

She wanted his kiss.

And she would have it—

A knock on the door halted everything. Startled Tad to such a degree that he jerked backward on the sofa, then off the furniture entirely as he jumped to his feet.

"Come," he said, the single word hoarse and jagged with his emotions.

Felicity, bless her, said nothing. And he didn't look to see her expression.

He didn't want to know if she was relieved at the interruption.

The door opened and a footman entered. "A visitor, sir. Mr. Greer. He is the neighbor to the east of Winterway House."

Tad stared at the servant incredulously, then looked down at his wife to find her pretending to read and biting her lip.

"Am I at home to visitors?" he asked, his voice catching on the words.

Felicity looked up from the book, her eyes gleaming with

humor. She gave him a helpless shrug when he frowned at her. She found the interruption amusing, it would seem.

"He is our neighbor," she said, raising her eyebrows, a smile playing at the corners of her lips. "And I cannot go about meeting all the ladies until their husbands and fathers have introduced themselves to you. Besides, Tad," she added, her voice dropping to a more intimate tone, "we will have plenty of time to continue our *conversation* later." She reached out, brushing his hand briefly with her own, a promise in her touch.

He felt the warmth of her fingers even after she withdrew, the lingering sensation both a comfort and a torment. Dash the gentry and their strange rules. He sighed and ran a hand through his hair, knowing that she was right, but still caught in the web of his longing.

"Show him to the sitting room on the ground floor. The blue one."

"Very good, sir." The footman bowed and left, as properly as he'd entered, and likely with no idea how close Tad had come to throttling him for the interruption.

Felicity picked up the book of poems with an innocent smile. She glanced at him from the corner of her eye. "You had best put your coat and boots back on, Tad."

"I suppose so." He picked up his coat with reluctance, pulling it on and adjusting his cravat. Then he scooped up his boots. Rather than sit beside her to put them on again, he bent closer. "I will find you later, then."

"I'm certain I will be about somewhere." The darling woman didn't look up from the book in her hands.

Indecision made him waver there. He wanted to take the book from her, toss it to the side, pull her into his arms, and finish what they'd nearly started. And the strength of those feelings frightened him.

Surely, a gentleman ought never handle a lady in such a way.

He sighed. Then kissed her forehead, the token no more than a brief press of his lips to her smooth, sweet skin. It was the most he would allow himself, and even then he worried he'd gone too far. He backed away, not looking to see how she received the affectionate gift. He went to the door and spoke once more, over his shoulder. "Stay here as long as you like. And please keep warm today."

Then he shut the door between them, his hand gripping the handle, feeling the cold brass and the weight of his own frustration. He bit back a groan, caught as it was between a sigh and a sound of longing.

They were man and wife, bound together by law, by circumstance, and by a growing connection that promised so much more. Yet, he was trapped by his own uncertainties, his own fears of overstepping. How could he be both a gentleman and a husband? How could he navigate the delicate dance of their newfound intimacy without faltering? He still felt like such a fool, a man caught between worlds, yearning for connection but terrified of the unknown.

Seven

F elicity was informed that the very man who unknowingly interrupted her kiss with Tad, was invited to dinner. Mr. Greer was a pleasant neighbor and an excellent—though unexpected—dinner guest. She'd done her best to treat him graciously, even though his presence during and after the meal meant she couldn't say a word to Tad about their almost-kiss.

The memory of the lost opportunity played at the edges of her mind near constantly.

When their guest finally took his leave, the two of them were at last alone in the drawing room. For the first time since their interrupted moment.

Tad extended his arm to Felicity, silently offering to escort her to her room. She gently rested her hand on his arm. Her mind led her in a dance between attraction and reservation.

"Felicity?" Tad's voice brought her out of her thoughts with a blush.

"Hm?" She looked up at him. The flickering candles in the

wall sconces along the corridor made the rugged lines of his profile stand out quite handsomely.

"I've found myself thinking of our time together in the study most of the day," Tad remarked, his voice soft and appreciative. "I was quite . . . distracted by the memory, in truth."

Felicity's cheeks warmed, and she looked down at the intricate patterns in the carpet beneath her feet. "Was it an unwelcome distraction?" she asked, not daring to meet his eyes. But her tongue was braver. "Because I thought on it too. And I was rather disappointed that our time together ended so soon."

His hand covered hers where it rested on his arm, drawing her gaze upward. His dark brown eyes were nearly black in the evening shadows. "As was I. And it took more will than I wish to admit for me to keep away the rest of the day. But I thought it best, to give you time."

She raised her eyebrows, not quite comprehending what he meant. Why did she need time? Why had he thought keeping away would give such a thing to her?

They reached her door, and Tad's eyes held hers in a shared silence. The world fell away, leaving only the two of them standing at the threshold of something profound.

"Felicity," Tad began, his voice laced with tenderness, "Your feelings, your comfort, mean everything to me. If there is anything you need, anything you wish to discuss, please know that I'm always willing to listen."

His sincerity touched her deeply, and Felicity placed a hand on his cheek. "I know, Tad. I trust you."

The words hung in the air between them, and she hoped he heard everything she meant but couldn't say. There were certain things a lady never *could* say in their world of proper behavior. Even if they were husband and wife, there were expectations, unwritten rules, of words never spoken aloud.

She wanted him to hear everything, though. That he heard her permission. Her longing. Her willingness. With slow and careful movements, Tad leaned down to kiss her forehead, his lips pressed there a moment longer than necessary.

She sensed in that gentle kiss a promise, a pledge of faith. Perhaps something even more profound that she didn't yet have the confidence to describe.

Before the courage to act left her, Felicity lifted herself upward on her toes and leaned into him. She tilted her head enough to slant her lips over his, feeling the warm, soft curve of his mouth against her own. And as fear that she'd erred crept into her thoughts, his arms came around her waist as he kissed her back. Fully. Beautifully. Passionately.

Her heart raced, and every inch of her body warmed and thrilled with his touch.

"Felicity," he said, whispering her name against her lips as they parted. His voice was a low groan. "It's only been a few days. I won't—" He backed away from her, but she caught his hand in hers before he fled completely.

"I trust you," she repeated, not breaking her gaze. With a last squeeze of his hand, Felicity stepped backward. Entered her room. Closed the door behind her.

Clara waited for her, cheerful as always. Oblivious to the emotions coursing through Felicity's heart, the thoughts whirling in her mind. Clara chatted freely about her day as she assisted Felicity. She dressed for bed, as she always did, but the night's routine felt anything but normal. She braided her hair, trying to stay calm, as Clara ran the warming pan across her sheets. Felicity slipped between the sheets, and her maid withdrew, leaving a low-burning fire and a single lamp burning beside the bed.

Eventually, when Felicity started to doubt it would ever

happen, a soft knock sounded at the door connecting her room to her husband's. Heat flooded her cheeks, and she pulled the blanket all the way up to her chin.

"Come in," she called with more confidence than she felt.

Her husband entered her room, his expression awash with uncertainty. His hair looked a mess, as though he'd been caught in a windstorm. He didn't wear shoes or stockings. No coat, waistcoat, or cravat. His shirt was open at the neck and half-untucked, as though he hadn't made up his mind whether he was putting things on or off.

She bit her bottom lip, amused, and feeling oddly tender toward him. He seemed more tentative than she was about their roles as husband and wife. He came to the side of her bed and looked down at her, rubbing the back of his neck.

"Perhaps we could talk." The tone of his suggestion, the words edged with jagged uncertainty, made her want to shiver.

She scooted a little more to the other side and opened the blanket in a silent invitation. He slid into that side of the bed, then avoided all eye contact with her.

His eyes on the flickering flames of the low-burning fire, Tad seemed lost in thought. Felicity's heart ached at his vulnerability, and she reached out to take his hand, intertwining their fingers.

"Tad?" she whispered with a gentle squeeze of his hand.

He looked at her then, his eyes searching hers, filled with a depth of emotion that made her breath catch. "I didn't wish to presume," he murmured. "I want you to know that I will never ask anything of you that you're not willing to give."

A warm smile spread across her lips, and she squeezed his hand reassuringly. "And I want you to know that I've felt safe and cared for in every moment we've spent together."

They sat there in silence for a moment, simply being with each other, the weight of their feelings a comforting presence.

Slowly, almost hesitantly, Tad shifted closer, his arm finding its way around her shoulders. Felicity nestled against him, her head resting on his chest, listening to the steady beat of his heart.

Time slowed as they rested like that together, two souls growing nearer, exploring the newfound territory of trust and affection. To Felicity, words seemed unnecessary; their hearts and stillness spoke a language of their own.

The room grew colder as the fire dwindled, but in Tad's arms, she found warmth and comfort. A peaceful drowsiness settled over her, and her eyelids grew heavy.

"Tad?" she murmured, her voice laced with sleep.

"Yes, my darling?" he answered, his voice rich with affection. The new endearment made her heart skip happily.

"Stay with me, like this?" she said, a gentle plea in her voice.

"Always," he whispered, pressing a soft kiss to her forehead. Forehead kisses were her new favorite things.

With that happy thought, she drifted off to sleep, wrapped in her husband's arms.

Eight

T ad stared contemplatively at the frosted window of the seamstress's shop, his wife within, his mind drifting back to the soft warmth of the morning. Waking with Felicity in his arms had been an experience filled with an intimacy he'd never known before. Her gentle breathing, the silken touch of her hair against his skin, the contentment in her eyes when she first awoke—every detail was etched in his memory, analyzed, and cherished.

He'd slid from her bed before she woke. He didn't think she would regret the night spent snuggled close to him, but he hadn't desired to cause her a moment's discomfort. He'd gone to her hearth and built up the fire, to warm her chamber before she woke. Then he'd glanced up at the painting, barely visible in the dim morning light.

The village, depicted on a snowy winter's day, had inspired him. He'd returned to his chambers to dress, then wrote an invitation to his wife that he slid beneath the door that joined their rooms. An invitation to join him in a visit to Lynford Hollow.

An hour later, the paper had returned beneath the door with a single word scrawled in her elegant hand. *Yes.*

He couldn't help but marvel at the profound shift in their relationship. What had begun as a marriage between strangers was blossoming into something he didn't have words for yet. The attraction he felt for his wife was both physical and emotional, a blend that he found satisfying and slightly disconcerting.

Movement on the snow-covered village green pulled him from his reverie. A group of younger children, no more than five or six years old, were attempting to build a snowman. Their excitement was evident, but their lack of success was equally clear. The snow didn't pack as it should, and their little hands struggled to shape it properly.

They had even rolled a large ball on the ground, meant to be the middle of the snowman, only to have it fall apart when they placed it atop another. There were three little boys in caps and mittens, and two little girls in shawls, attempting the work.

Across the green, a cluster of older children industriously built a snow hut, laughing and chatting amongst themselves. They seemed oblivious to the younger ones' plight, or perhaps simply indifferent.

Tad noted the dynamics of the situation, and the challenges the younger children faced. His mind concluded that they didn't have enough experience to complete their task. Not without guidance. His heart couldn't help responding to their determination and frustration.

With a glance back at the shop, ensuring that Felicity remained engaged within, he made his decision. Crossing the road, he approached the children with a friendly smile.

"Good afternoon, ladies and gentlemen," he greeted, putting as much friendliness into his words as possible. He swept off his hat and bowed as they froze where they stood. "It seems you could use a helping hand with your snowman. May I offer my assistance?"

The children looked up at him, eyes wide and faces flushed from the cold. One of the little girls narrowed her eyes at him.

"But you're Mr. Harcourt."

"I am," he agreed. "And you are?"

She looked to her friends, but when they all stared silently back at her, she shrugged and pulled her shawl tighter about her shoulders. "Ellen. And this is Beth, Harry, Jack, and Edward."

The children all bobbed their best formal greetings.

"A pleasure to meet all of you. Now that we've had proper introductions, may I join you?"

After a moment's hesitation, they broke into smiles, and eagerly accepted his offer.

Tad bent down, his large hands more capable than theirs, and shaped the snow. The children gathered around him, their excitement renewed, as they worked together to create a large ball the size of a boulder.

"All of us should roll it together," he told them. "We need the bottom section to be as large as we can make it. And packed tight."

Had he built a snowman even once in his life? Not that he could recall. But he'd seen others do so, and the principles were simple.

They giggled and tripped from time to time, but the foundation of the snowman was soon completed, and they began work on the midsection. Round and round they went, rolling the ball until it grew to just the right size. Tad had to lift it, and then the children started on the head without him.

He watched them with a grin, and he realized the older group of children had paused in their work to stare across the snow-covered green. He raised his hand in a wave, and one of the older boys returned the gesture enthusiastically. He recognized Jeremiah, the lad who had watched his horse during their last visit to the village.

The boy jogged over, snow flying up behind his shoes.

"Mr. Harcourt," he said with a foggy puff of air leaving his lungs. "Sir, what are you doing?"

"Building a snowman." He waved to the children to catch their attention. "I think the head is large enough now."

One of the boys tried to lift it and grunted. "It's too heavy, Mr. Harcourt."

"I'll help." Jeremiah jogged over and lifted the head, stumbling a bit before he walked it over to Tad.

"Thank you." Tad accepted the ball and put it atop the other two. "Excellent work. Now, I believe one usually gives such a creation arms. Buttons for his snow coat too. Perhaps even eyes and a smile?"

The children scattered, including Jeremiah back to his group of friends. A moment later, and the older children were digging in the snow beneath a large oak tree. Likely coming up with branches and round stones. Perhaps acorns.

"What about a fine hat?" a voice asked.

Immediate tenderness swept over Tad at the sound. He turned to see Felicity coming across the road, one hand in her muff and the other holding a large-brimmed straw hat that had seen better days.

"Where did you find that horrible thing?" he asked, crossing his arms and watching her approach.

"Horrible thing?" she repeated, her jaw dropping. "I am affronted, sir. This horrible thing, as you say, is a very fine old hat. Donated by the milliner." She strode up to the snowman and put the hat atop the rounded head. "And look at that. It's a perfect fit."

He pretended to examine the snowman, walking around it. "Hm. I'm not certain it's dignified enough."

"You could always give the snowy fellow *your* hat," she proposed, putting her free hand on her hip, a challenge in her eyes. Her lips twitched as she resisted the urge to smile.

The children returned, both large and small, and Tad stepped back while they debated which sticks would make for the best arms. Which acorns the best buttons and eyes. And when they realized how many more potential limbs and such they had, someone suggested they make more snow folk.

"Will you help us, Mr. Harcourt?" Ellen, the first little girl daring enough to speak to him, asked with wide eyes and a pleading glance directed first to him and then to his wife. "And your missus too."

Felicity grinned at him. "It sounds as though we have a duty to perform, dearest."

His heart fluttered, and he gave a firm nod. "All right. We will populate the village with snow people."

The children cheered and everyone went to work. Felicity seemed quite adept at the process, chatting with the little girls as they formed smaller balls to join together, creating snow children to gather around near their larger kin.

He'd never had such fun before, not even as a child. Hearing the children laugh and talk with one another, and watching his wife giggle at their antics and praise them by turns, made the afternoon one he would never forget.

With a satisfied smile, he placed the final touch on the last snowman, standing back to admire their handiwork. The children cheered, their faces alight with joy, and Tad felt a warmth inside that kept him from feeling winter's chill.

He noticed that his wife's nose had turned pink, and several of the children were stomping their shoes and rubbing their hands together to keep warm. He looked at Jeremiah and pushed his hat back slightly.

"Jeremiah, do you think your father would serve a group of fine builders some warm cider and rolls?"

The little ones gasped while the older children grinned at their friend.

"I think he'd like to give us a treat," the boy said with a large grin.

"Then we're all off to The Hollow's Hearth." Tad bent to pick up the smallest child, the little girl called Beth, and put her on his shoulders. She wore the least serviceable shoes, and her teeth were near to chattering. He'd found out one of the older children was her brother, tasked with looking after her. The boy had likely forgotten to check that his sister was warm enough. A stop at the tavern would set the child to rights.

Felicity bestowed a beautiful, admiring smile on Tad before she took Ellen's hand and led the way. They strode in parade-fashion across the road and down the row of shops until they came to the public house. The children stepped inside, and the warmth of the building's multiple hearths stung as it hit Tad's cold cheeks.

"Innkeeper," Tad said with a raised voice. "I'd like to buy these fine children cider, rolls, and any biscuits you have on hand. They've worked hard and deserve a treat."

Jeremiah's father, who'd been tidying up a table, was a man of large stature and an even larger grin.

"At once, Mr. Harcourt. Jeremiah, lad, come help me in the kitchen. We mustn't delay."

The children rushed to the hearth, pulling off mittens and caps to hang on the hooks just above it. Chattering happily. He swung the little girl from his shoulders to the floor, and she gave him a shy thank you before scampering away to join the others.

The older boys dragged a bench from along the wall to sit directly before the fire.

Felicity sidled up to him, her cheeks now pinker than her nose. "I am beginning to suspect I have a very fine husband, Mr. Harcourt."

He glanced down at her, arms crossed over his chest. "Really?" He raised his eyebrows. "Why would you even think such a preposterous thing?"

"Do you know what you did today?"

"I built a bevy of snowmen," he said with a grin. "Best fun I've had in ages, too."

She leaned closer to him, her shoulder brushing his arm. "You did more than that. You sowed seeds of kindness, trust, and empathy. These children will remember this afternoon for ages. And the older ones might be quicker to help the younger, in future."

He lowered his gaze to the ground. "I saw the little ones struggling and suppose I had sympathy for their plight. I must admit, though, I enjoyed myself tremendously. I don't think I've ever spent that much time playing in snow."

"You were quite marvelous at it." She leaned her head against his arm briefly, a teasing smile on her lips that made him remember the kiss from the night before. He'd been too stunned, too shy, when he woke beside her that morning to try for another. He regretted that now. He certainly couldn't claim such a token while they were in public.

Settling at a table near the children, Tad and Felicity enjoyed cider of their own. After the tavern keeper assured Felicity that the little ones had a far milder concoction than what the adults enjoyed. Not long after they arrived, two mothers appeared in search of their children. Felicity introduced herself to the blacksmith's wife and the cobbler's daughter. The other children seemed content to stay near the fire, and Jeremiah assured Tad and Felicity it was all right.

They ought to take leave as well. He looked one last time the children as they laughed and talked of the snow. They'd given him something more than a moment of play. The appreciation that settled in his heart made him warm throughout, doing a better job than the cider had to chase the cold from his limbs.

They bid the children farewell, and Tad led his wife back into the winter sunlight. Making their way to their vehicle, they passed the snowmen, and Tad noted the snowman with Felicity's straw hat faced the lane. Even with an old, misshapen hat, the snowman wore a smile. Thanks to cleverly placed pebbles and the children.

The marvelous afternoon had happened because of a shopping trip.

"Did you arrange for a gown?" he asked his wife, helping her into the carriage. If it snowed again, they'd need to switch to the sleigh to visit the village.

Felicity's eyes sparkled with delight. "A beautiful one, I think. I wish I had already owned something appropriate, but for so long all I have worn is gray and black. And even before..." She wilted briefly. "Well, there was no point to a fine gown. Not for years, with Grandmother's poor health."

"Felicity," he said, wrapping his hand around hers. "Commission all the gowns you wish. You deserve lovely things." He was grateful he could now provide such things for her, after all she'd been through losing both her grandmother and parents. He ached to give her everything.

Her cheeks turned pink, and she lowered her gaze to their joined hands. "Thank you, Tad."

When they arrived home, Tad and Felicity had barely entered the house when a footman came forward with a letter. "I beg your pardon, Mr. Harcourt, but this letter arrived by special courier whilst you were away."

Tad exchanged a curious glance with his wife before he released her hand and accepted the note. He recognized the handwriting at once, and the bold strokes of the pen told him in what mood the missive had been sent. He released a heavy sigh.

FELICITY WATCHED AS TAD BROKE THE WAX SEAL, A frown creasing his brow as he read through the lines of his letter. She could sense a change in the air, a ripple of tension that settled over the room and her husband.

"What is it, Tad?" she asked, concern growing inside of her.

"It's from Father," he replied, his tone edged with frustration. "He's in London, managing some business affairs, and it seems there are some complications. Complications he lays at my door. He thought I had taken care of an important matter with one of our clients before our marriage. But I told him . . ." His voice trailed away as his brow furrowed, his eyes still on the letter.

Felicity came closer, laying her hand on his arm. "Is it serious?"

He grimaced. "No. At least, it won't be once I've clarified things." He folded the paper and put it into his coat. "I need to attend to this at once. Will you be all right?"

"Of course." She had dozens of duties to see to, especially given the coming ball. There were invitations to pen, orders to send to the village, and menus to plan. "I think I can distract myself suitably."

Her husband didn't seem to hear her. He had already turned away, shaking his head as he went for the staircase. He would go to his study, she supposed. To the copies of ledgers for his father's business.

Felicity soon found herself settled in the drawing room with Mrs. Bennet, a stack of invitations and a list of names spread across the table. The sun streamed through the windows, casting a cheerful glow over the room, but Felicity's heart felt heavy.

"Lady Felicity, what do you think about including the Wentworths?" Mrs. Bennet asked, her voice bright and expectant. "They've recently returned from their travels to Austria, and I think it would be a lovely gesture. They were good friends with the Deerwoods."

Felicity's gaze drifted to the window, her thoughts consumed by the image of Tad, shoulders hunched as he'd walked away from her, his face lined with concern. She blinked and forced her attention back to the task at hand.

"Yes, the Wentworths would be a wonderful addition," she replied, her voice full of enthusiasm she didn't quite feel.

Mrs. Bennet's sharp eyes caught Felicity's distraction. "Is everything all right, my lady?" she inquired, leaning slightly forward in her chair.

Felicity shook her head, trying to dispel her unease. "I'm concerned about Mr. Harcourt. That letter from his father put him out of sorts so quickly."

Mrs. Bennet reached across the table, patting Felicity's hand. "I haven't known him long, but Mr. Harcourt seems to be a capable man. He will manage, I'm sure. Now, let's focus on our task. What about the Ashfords? And perhaps the Ellingtons?"

Felicity nodded, trying to immerse herself in the details of the guest list. But her mind kept drifting back to Tad, imagining him alone in his study, burdened by his father's expectations. She found herself adding names to the list absently, her thoughts elsewhere.

As the afternoon turned to evening, and she completed each of her tasks, Felicity's worry deepened. As she dressed for dinner, she caught herself glancing at the door, half-expecting Tad to appear, his face bright with triumph at having resolved his business dilemma.

But the door between their rooms remained closed, and the silence of the house seemed to echo her own uncertainty.

Clara put the finishing touches on Felicity's hair, her own mood subdued by her mistress's solemn contemplation.

A knock at the door startled them both. But it hadn't come from Tad's room. It was from the corridor.

Clara answered the knock to find a footman there.

"Mr. Harcourt sends his regrets to Lady Felicity, but he won't be at the dining table this evening."

Felicity turned in her chair to look at the man, questions rising to her lips. Questions a servant wouldn't know the answer to, or at least would have no business answering. She gripped the chair she sat in and forced a grateful smile. "Thank you, Thompson. Has a tray been taken to his study?"

"Yes, my lady."

"Have one sent up to me, too, please," she said. He bowed and disappeared.

Felicity looked up at Clara, the false smile still in place. "I suppose we must undo all your hard work."

Her maid gave her a rather uncertain frown. "Are you well, Lady Felicity?"

Felicity forced a chuckle, though it was doubtful Clara believed her. "I'm perfectly well. Merely tired. Did I tell you we played in the snow with the village children today?"

She distracted herself recounting their time building snowmen. But her heart was heavy, and her thoughts were with Tad. The joy and excitement of their night spent together and their lovely afternoon seemed overshadowed by the sudden intrusion of doubt and worry, and Felicity felt a pang of longing for the simplicity and certainty of being in his arms.

As she ate her dinner alone, curled up in the chair near her fire, she gazed up at the painting. Then narrowed her eyes and stood, drawing as close as she could to inspect it, her hands resting gently on the mantel.

The snow hadn't been so deep on the village ground before, had it? And there, at the corner of the painting—where the village green would be if the painting was larger—that rounded shape. She shook her head. Of course it wasn't a snowman. She would have noticed one before now, surely. And one of the windows now glowed yellow with light from within. And a small face peered out of it. A child's face, smiling at the snow.

The clock directly in front of her chimed, and Felicity nearly leaped out of her slippers from surprise. She covered her pounding heart with one hand and laughed. "Don't be silly," she said aloud, glancing at the child's visage in the corner of the painted window. "Of course those things were always there. Paintings do not change with the weather."

She resumed eating her dinner, then tried to read. Waiting for Tad.

Hours later, she left her chair. Her nightgown covered in a wrap, and her warm slippers on her feet, she picked up a lamp and went in search of her husband.

She found him in his study, his coat off and hair disheveled, fully absorbed in the papers and ledgers on his desk.

"Tad?"

He didn't look up. "Yes?" Then he blinked, as though he realized only one person now called him by that name. He stood abruptly, his chair scraping the floor. "Felicity. What are you doing up still?" He looked up at the clock on the mantel. "It's nearly midnight."

"I know." She came deeper into the room. "I came to see if you needed anything. Such as convincing to come to bed." She let the hope show in her smile.

He heaved a deep sigh and looked down at the desk again. "I need to finish this. I won't be able to sleep until I've sorted out the mess."

"What happened?" She put her lamp down on the table near the sofa. "Is there any way I can help?"

He shook his head. "No. Shipments didn't go where they were supposed to. Apologies must be written. Orders must be redirected." He lowered himself back into his chair and picked up a piece of paper.

"Tad, it will be all right. You can manage it," Felicity reassured, attempting to break through his sudden withdrawal.

"You should go to bed," he said, glancing up with a weak smile. His eyes were rimmed with red. "I will be at this most of the night."

Felicity hesitated, the cold chill of the room seeming to creep into her bones.

"But perhaps I could—" she started, her voice soft and uncertain.

"No," he replied, not looking up. "I need to concentrate."

Felicity's heart ached at his dismissal, but she persisted. "Perhaps I can just sit here, read a book, keep you company. I won't be a distraction."

Tad looked up, his eyes meeting hers for a fleeting moment before returning to his papers. "Felicity, I appreciate the offer, but I need to be alone."

A heavy silence settled over the room. Felicity felt a pang of rejection, her chest tightening. She moved closer, laying her hand gently on his shoulder. "Tad, it's late. You look exhausted. Can't it wait until morning?"

He stiffened under her touch, his pen pausing in its frantic dance across the paper. "I told you, it needs to be done now." His voice was strained, the edges of frustration sharpening his words.

Felicity's hand lingered, the warmth of his body beneath her fingers a stark contrast to the coldness in his voice. "But surely, a break, some rest—"

"No!" he snapped, the word slicing through the room like a blade. He pushed his chair back, standing abruptly. "Please," he said, the word brimming with agitation. "Leave me to my work."

Felicity recoiled, her hand falling to her side. The room seemed to shrink, the walls closing in. She searched his eyes for a hint of the man who had built snowmen with her, but all she saw was a stranger, distant and unapproachable.

"Good night, then," she said, her voice barely above a whisper. He mumbled a response, his attention already back on his work.

Felicity retreated, her steps heavy, her heart aching. The door closed behind her with a soft click, with a finality that made her wince. She climbed into her cold, empty bed, disliking the sudden uncertainty that had entered her heart. And for the first time since her marriage, her thoughts were shadowed with doubt.

Nine

F elicity sat in the drawing room, absently playing with the lace on her sleeves as she tried to shake the unease that had settled over her. The house was unusually quiet, a stillness that seemed to mirror her troubled thoughts. She knew that Tad had worked until dawn and was now resting, but the cold dismissal of the previous night still stung. She felt a confusing mixture of concern, rejection, and doubt.

A knock at the door interrupted her thoughts, and she looked up to find Mrs. Bennet entering, a strained smile on her face.

"Your ladyship, Lady Victoria Wainwright has come calling," Mrs. Bennet announced, her voice tinged with hesitation.

Felicity had met Lady Victoria Wainwright only once in London, years before her grandmother's illness. Everyone knew the earl's daughter had a sharp tongue and haughty demeanor. Her family held an ancient title, and she never let anyone forget it. Felicity's stomach twisted, but she rose and nodded, steeling herself.

Lady Victoria had married a gentleman who lived five miles

north of Winterway House. Apparently, five miles wasn't enough to keep her away.

"Please show her in," Felicity said, forcing a gracious smile.

Lady Victoria swept into the drawing room, her silks rustling, her nose tilted ever so slightly upward. She was older than Felicity, her beauty mature and her eyes shrewd.

"My dear Lady Felicity," she cooed, her voice dripping with false warmth. "How are you faring in these . . . interesting times?"

Felicity greeted her with a polite curtsy, choosing to ignore the undertones in Lady Victoria's words. "I'm well, thank you. Please, make yourself comfortable."

They settled into the ornate chairs, and Felicity ordered tea. Their brief exchange on the weather, on the health of their families, was stilted, the undercurrents of judgment palpable.

"Tell me, dear," Lady Victoria said after accepting her tea, her eyes narrowing slightly, "how do you find married life with a merchant's son? I must say, it was quite the surprise when I heard you had married into the Harcourt family. My cousin wrote me all about it."

Lord William Thursby and Lady Victoria were, indeed, cousins. Thick as thieves, too, from what their grandmother used to say during Felicity's visits with her grandmother.

Felicity's cheeks warmed, but she kept her voice steady. "Mr. Harcourt is a wonderful man, and we are very happy."

Lady Victoria's lips quirked into a condescending smile. "Of course, dear. But you must admit, it's a different world you've entered, isn't it? I mean, marrying into trade. If one is going to marry a mere *Mister*, she ought to consider a landowner of some reputation. As I did."

Felicity's fingers tightened around her teacup, the insinuations in Lady Victoria's words striking uncomfortably close to her current fears. The fears that she didn't understand her husband so well as she ought to, to be a good wife to him.

"Every marriage is an entry into a new world," Felicity replied, her voice calm. "But my husband isn't a merchant any longer, of course. He has left that behind him." But he hadn't. Not really. And she wasn't certain why anyone would think he should. "He is a gentleman, with holdings that ensure our future comfort."

Lady Victoria's eyes gleamed with amusement, her voice turning syrupy sweet. "Oh, I have no doubt the Harcourt holdings are impressive. But people from such different backgrounds . . . one can't help but wonder if misunderstandings are inevitable. He was not born to his station, and you were born a step above it."

Felicity's heart pounded, the snobbish comment echoing the doubts that had been gnawing at her since last night.

"He doesn't lack for his upbringing. Not in any way. My husband is a perfect gentleman in manner and character. Beyond that concern, I believe understanding comes from the heart, not one's background," Felicity said, her voice firm.

Lady Victoria simpered at her, her eyes glinting with something Felicity couldn't quite place. "Well, dear, I certainly hope you are right."

They moved on to other topics, but the barbs of Lady Victoria's comments hung in the air like a fog, seeping into Felicity's soul. When the visit finally ended, and Lady Victoria had swept from the room, Felicity was left in somber contemplation, the shadows of doubt and worry deepening.

Felicity moved to the window that overlooked the front of the estate, watching Lady Victoria's carriage pull away. Still troubled by their conversation. The afternoon sun was losing its warmth, obscured by clouds that threatened rain.

Was there truth in Lady Victoria's words? Had she and Tad misunderstood each other? The question wore at her, the seeds of uncertainty taking root, threatening to grow and overshadow the tender affection that had begun to bloom between them.

She absently traced the edge of the carpet near the window with her slipper. Then paused when something caught her eye. The corner of a piece of paper stuck out from beneath the edge of the heavy rug. Curiosity piqued, she bent and tugged it free, surprised to find a note in a bold, masculine hand:

To My Dearest C.,

Every day I am grateful for your love and your patience with my imperfections. Your grace and understanding make me a better man. You are my heart, and your love is my salvation.

Forever yours, N. Deerwood

Felicity's lips curved into an amused smile as she read the words. How sweet and earnest they were! The note was a testament to enduring love, to forgiveness and understanding, even in the face of difficulties.

She looked out at the gathering clouds again, but now they seemed less ominous, less threatening. The Deerwoods' love had weathered storms, and so could hers. She folded the note and placed it back where she found it, a secret treasure hidden away, a reminder that love could be resilient, forgiving, and unbreakable.

She would talk to Tad that evening. Even apologize for being stubborn the evening before, while he had been obviously distracted by an important matter. Her heart felt lighter, her resolve strengthened. Love was not something easily shattered; it was something to be nurtured, tended, and understood.

And she knew, in her heart, that she and Tad had the strength to do exactly that.

TAD AWOKE WITH A START, THE ROOM ENVELOPED IN A dull gray light. Disquiet settled over him, a nagging feeling that something was wrong. Rubbing his eyes, the memory of last night's harsh words came rushing back.

Felicity coming into his study. Trying to help. And he'd dismissed her, curtly.

Though not at first. Though he barely remembered what he'd said when he became aware of her standing near him. Then she'd left quietly. After he'd denied the need of her assistance multiple times.

Why hadn't she listened after his first answer?

With that thought, a sharp memory punctured his present thoughts. The memory of being a boy, barely able to see over his father's desk. Putting his hands on its edge to look across the stacks of paper and books.

"Can I help you do your work, Papa?"

The response was a dismissive wave. "No. You'd only be in the way."

"Please? I could fetch you a cup of tea. Or stack your books. Or—"

With a cold glare and deep frown, his father's snapped, "Why don't you listen to me the first time I tell you a thing, Theodore? You are being a nuisance. Be gone with you. I have important work to do."

He'd slunk away. Feeling like an unwanted interruption instead of a cherished son.

His heart twisted at the realization of what he'd done. Guilt washed over him, and he made his way to the window, pulling back the curtain. Icy rain was falling from a leaden sky, casting the world in a dark and dreary hue.

Dressed and driven by a need to make amends, he found Felicity in a small sitting room, sewing. Her back to him, she seemed lost in thought, and his heart ached to mend the rift he had created.

"Felicity?" he said softly.

She turned, her face pale, her surprise giving way to a guarded expression. "Tad. You're awake. How are you feeling?"

"I'm sorry, Felicity. For last night," he said, stepping closer, his voice earnest. "I had no right to speak to you that way."

Lips parting, Felicity stared at him with silent surprise.

"I knew after waking this morning that it was wrong. I behaved poorly."

Her eyes softened slightly, but she looked away. "It's quite all right, Tad. You were tired, frustrated. I understand. I ought to apologize for not listening—"

He shook his head, moving closer. "No, Felicity. Don't. You were only being considerate and kind. But I wasn't either of those things in the way I snapped at you last night. It is I who owe you an apology."

She looked up at him, her eyes glistening. "It isn't really necessary."

"But it is." He reached out, taking her hands in his. "I want to understand you, Felicity. And I want you to understand me. Understand that I will do my best to keep my words kind, no matter the circumstance. Please. Will you forgive me?"

"Of course I will, Tad."

Felicity's smile was tentative as she accepted his apology. The hurt in her eyes seemed gone, but a shadow there told him she was still guarded. It was a fragile thing, this newfound bond between them, and he knew he needed to tread carefully. His father's gruff manner and the way he treated his family loomed in Tad's mind, a stark warning. He would not follow that path.

Though feelings were neutralized, things hadn't returned to normal. He needed to see her laugh again, to bring back the levity and lightness from before he had snapped at her.

"I suppose we should make the best of this, shouldn't we?" he said, attempting to lighten the mood with a teasing smile. "After all, it's not every day a woman gets such a sincere apology from such a dashing merchant."

Felicity looked at him, her brow arching, a hint of amusement in her eyes. "Dashing merchant? My, someone thinks highly of himself."

He chuckled, pleased to see her mood lifting. "And what about you, my lady? The spirited daughter of an earl, gracing a simple merchant with her presence?"

She laughed now, the sound musical and warm, washing away the last of the tension. "Spirited? I don't think anyone has ever called me that before." She tilted her head to the side, studying him. "Perhaps we both have much to learn about each other, Mr. Harcourt."

"Perhaps we do, Lady Felicity," he said, his voice soft, the promise unspoken but understood. He would endeavor never to speak to her harshly again. He settled into the chair nearest hers. "Ask me anything."

"Oh dear. Anything? That makes it difficult to decide on a topic. Let me see." She tapped her lips with one slender finger. "If you could meet anyone from history, who would you like to meet?"

Tad released a quick laugh. "What?"

"It is a nonsensical question, but I think it interesting. For instance, I would like to meet Mary, Queen of Scots. I have dozens of questions I would ask her about what she thought of her cousin Elizabeth." The way her eyes lit with interest made his heart soften.

"Such an interview would be a priceless experience." He tilted his head to the side, studying the way light from the window bathed her in a gentle glow. She was lovely.

"I read Cary's translation of *Dante's Inferno*. Against my grandmother's wishes, I'm afraid." Her cheeks pinked with the admission. "And I thought that if he could meet all sorts of famous people in the afterlife, I would want to do the same."

"Hopefully not in the same location as Dante." His teasing made her smile and the pink deepened. "Let me think a moment. Who would I like to meet?" He hummed a note as he thought, tapping his fingers on the arm of the chair. "I have it. Alfred the Great."

"An interesting choice. Why him?" She had resumed her embroidery of a handkerchief, but glanced up at him with raised eyebrows and a challenge in her smile.

"Many reasons. Alfred was a warrior king, but he was more than that, too. He was a patron of the arts, literature, and education. He initiated a cultural and educational revival, bringing scholars from other parts of Europe to his court and teaching his people to value reading and study. Our earliest sources even name him as the founder of Oxford. I think any conversation with such a man would prove fascinating."

"You have a great respect for education," she noted aloud. "This isn't the first time you've mentioned an admiration for scholars."

It was his turn to blush, though he wasn't entirely certain why. Except—no. He knew why. "My father was insistent I attain the education of a gentleman, even before he had the means to set me up as one. He was adamant about it." Tad lowered his gaze to the arm of his chair, realizing he'd gripped it tightly the moment he thought of his father. He released his hold with a shake of his head. "But he also declared the study of art and history a waste of time. He didn't see any use for it, except as a way of having conversations that the working class man could never hope to understand."

"That is a rather harsh perspective. Though I suppose there are not many of the merchant class who have studied Da Vinci. Or Alfred the Great."

When he raised his gaze to hers, he found sympathy in her smile. He relaxed somewhat. "My mother taught me to read. She told me, when I was protesting the idea of learning my letters, that a man who could read could unlock the ability to learn *anything*. Because he could read every book on any subject he wished. She must've told me the same thing hundreds of times."

"I wish I could know your mother better," Felicity said, voice soft. "She was so kind to me when we met. Do you think they will come for Christmas? I had written again to ask, but your mother's response still expressed uncertainty."

Another sharp pain in his mind made him wince. He pushed away the memories this time, though, rather than relive them. Instead, he answered his wife's question. "I doubt they will come. My father never saw the use of Christmas. It is only another day to manage accounts and write correspondence."

The way her expression changed from carefully hoping to outright disappointment made him wish to take the words back. Or go to London himself to drag his family's coach to the countryside for Christmas celebrations.

"That must have been a difficult thing, to not mark the day. I know there are many who see no reason to celebrate. But my grandmother always tried to make the day special. Perhaps next year we can travel to London and have Christmas with your mother, and then your father needn't give up the day of business for travel."

His wife was too lovely, too kind, too wonderful a woman.

"She would like that. But what of your hope to carry on the traditions the Deerwoods started?"

"Perhaps the traditions will need adjustment." She shrugged her shoulders and looked down at her embroidery hoop. "The people in our present are far more important than traditions of the past."

His adoration of her grew, and he knew not what to say. Thankfully, she brought up the topic of the ball again, explaining what preparations she had yet to make.

They spent the next hour in pleasant conversation, sharing stories, learning more about each other's lives and dreams. The connection between them deepening with every word, slowly and gently.

As the afternoon turned to evening, Tad stood, extending his hand. "Shall we have dinner, my lady? I promise to make my company as pleasant as possible."

She took his hand, her lovely smile making his pulse jump. "I think I would like that very much."

He led her to her room so she could dress for dinner. His heart lighter, he rushed through his own change of clothes, knowing they were on the right path. But the memory of his father's ways couldn't be dispelled. Samuel Harcourt had always let business come first, and Tad had done the same. He would be different; he would be careful. He owed it to Felicity, and he owed it to himself.

As they sat down to dinner, the icy rain still falling outside, Tad was acutely aware that they were starting something new. Something special. A relationship that was theirs to nurture, to grow.

He looked down the long table at his wife and heaved a purposefully loud sigh. "This will never do."

She appeared somewhat startled. "Is the first course not to your liking?"

"The food is perfect. But this—" He gestured between them. "This vast expanse of oak between us isn't to be borne."

The woman on the other end lowered her fork and knife to the table, then daintily patted her lips with her napkin. "Are you suggesting I move, sir?"

"Never." He rose. "I'm not certain about other gentlemen, but I couldn't ask such a thing of you, my lady." He picked up his plate, and the two footmen attending to the meal rushed forward to gather the rest of his place setting as he moved to sit in the empty chair on Felicity's right. Her eyes widened and her lips parted in surprise, but Tad settled in the chair as though it was where he'd belonged all along.

As the cups and cutlery were arranged around him, Tad grinned at his wife without a hint of shame. "Thank you, Thompson and Rigby," he said to the footmen as they withdrew again.

He glanced at Felicity, noting the way the candlelight danced in her eyes. "You know, dear wife, it occurs to me that we've been quite formal with each other this evening. Might we entertain some playful banter over dinner?"

The surprise in her expression faded to amusement. "Playful banter, Mr. Harcourt? I didn't think people suggested such a thing. I thought it merely happened."

"Ah, so bringing it up is something of a *faux pas*. I apologize. Silly me." He was making a fool of himself, but he didn't care. After the previous evening, she deserved to laugh. Even if it was at him.

She took up her fork and knife again. "Perhaps we might try something else. I can be quite the adversary in a battle of wits."

Tad raised an eyebrow, his lips curling into a mischievous

smile. "A battle of wits, you say? I'm intrigued. Shall we start with a wager then?"

Felicity leaned forward, narrowing her eyes at him. "A wager? I'm listening."

"If I can guess your favorite dessert, you must tell me a secret about yourself. Something you've never told anyone."

Felicity's laughter filled the room, and she shook her head. "Oh, that's a lovely idea. But if you fail, you must share a secret with me."

Tad's eyes sparkled with delight. "I agree to your terms."

"Fruit tart," Tad announced triumphantly as dessert was served.

Felicity's eyes widened, but she shook her head. "Not at all specific enough. You must guess which sort of fruit."

He grinned and leaned closer to her, ignoring the quickening of his heart. "Blackberry."

Her lovely pink lips parted in surprise. "How did you know?"

"I pay attention, my lady. Do you not recall picking up a tart the morning of our wedding, at the breakfast table? You declared it your favorite. And it was blackberry. Now, your secret?"

She blushed, her voice dropping to a whisper. "When I was a child, I used to visit the edge of the wood, pretending I was a fairy who had to gather acorn caps for all the other fairies."

Tad's laughter joined hers, the sound rich and warm. "What a delightful secret. I promise it's safe with me." And the oak tree, tucked in the corner of their garden would have acorns. Perhaps he would bring her a few of their caps.

They continued to eat, exchanging playful jabs, guessing favorite colors, childhood memories, and even sharing silly stories. Each revelation brought them closer, the laughter easing the tension that had loomed between them. The icy rain outside seemed distant now, forgotten in the warmth of her company.

Tad reached across the table, taking her hand. "I must confess, Felicity, this evening has been enchanting."

She squeezed his hand, her smile soft and her cheeks turning pink. "I missed your company last evening. But, Tad. I do understand that there must be times when you are too busy, or when your responsibilities call you away."

"I know. Thank you for that." He released her hand as the servants brought in dessert, and both of them burst out laughing when they saw the arrangement of blueberry tarts and spiced pears.

They spoke more over the fruit, the conversation flowing effortlessly. Tad couldn't remember an evening spent in so perfect a manner. It was a night he would remember, a turning point in their relationship. His wife was a marvel.

But he had to be careful with her heart, because carelessness on his part could ruin everything.

Ten

The ride to the Moore's residence the following Sunday evening was quiet, the gentle sway of the carriage allowing Felicity time to reflect on the changes of the last few days. The icy rain had given way to a clear, brisk day, and the world seemed washed clean. She felt a similar cleansing in her own heart, a thawing that came with Tad's heartfelt apology and his renewed kindness.

The previous night had been different. They had shared her bed again, but this time there was no underlying tension, no unspoken expectations. They had simply sought warmth in each other's presence, a mutual understanding that allowed them both to rest peacefully. Felicity found herself relieved, content in the innocence of their companionship.

Earlier, they had attended church, sitting together in the pews, their hands occasionally brushing as they shared the hymnal. Felicity had looked over at Tad during the sermon, noting the thoughtful expression on his face. He seemed a man committed to personal growth, to being better. His apology and promise to her had been made with such sincerity, she hadn't doubted it for an instant.

She found herself admiring him, not just for his apology but for the sincerity in his efforts to understand her, to make her comfortable.

Now, as they approached the reverend's home, she felt a flutter of anticipation. Mr. Moore and his wife, Eliza, were respected members of the community, and this dinner was an opportunity for her and Tad to come to know their new community better. She wondered how he would interact with the reverend, how he would fit into this social setting.

Tad glanced at her, a warm smile on his face. "Nervous?"

"A little," she admitted, smiling back. "I've never dined with a reverend before."

He gave her hand a reassuring squeeze. "You'll be fine. The Moores are kind people."

She nodded, feeling a surge of gratitude for his support. They were in this together, navigating the complexities of their relationship, learning to trust and depend on each other.

The carriage pulled up to the Moore's home, and Tad helped her down, his hand strong and steady.

Reverend Moore and his wife, Eliza, greeted them warmly, introducing them to two other couples from the community: Mr. and Mrs. Thornton, a distinguished older pair, and Mr. and Mrs. Edwards, a younger couple not much older than Felicity herself. The dining room was aglow with soft candlelight, the table set with elegant plates and silverware.

Conversation flowed easily, touching on local events, the weather, and the recent happenings in town. Felicity found herself enchanted by the hospitality and the kindness of their hosts and fellow guests.

Dinner was a delightful affair, each course a testament to the

Moores' fine taste and the cook's culinary skill. Felicity soon relaxed, drawn into the lively discussions and the friendly banter.

As the dinner conversation drifted towards local history, Felicity sensed an opportunity to satisfy her curiosity about Winterway House's previous owners. She turned her attention to Mr. Edwards, who had said moments before he had lived in the community his entire life.

"Mr. Edwards," she began, leaning slightly toward the man. "I've been so charmed by the entire Winterway Estate. I've heard mention of its previous owners, the Deerwoods, but only in passing. Might you know something more of them?"

A thoughtful look crossed Mr. Edwards's face, his eyes distant as he recalled memories from his youth. "I knew them when I was a child. Mrs. Deerwood was a particularly kind soul. She used to visit all the houses in the neighborhood, rich and poor alike, always bringing biscuits for the children. She knew all of us by name too."

"What, all the children in the community?" Tad asked, eyebrows rising. It seemed all eyes now were on her conversation with Mr. Edwards.

"She treated everyone with respect. Noticed everyone," Mr. Edwards added with a shrug. "Her husband as well. He would play marbles with us sometimes. And there was one summer when he put on a Punch and Judy show for us at the village green."

Felicity laughed. "I used to love Punch and Judy."

Mr. Thornton chuckled. "Doesn't every child? There is nothing so ridiculous as a puppetry show. Deerwood never hesitated to make people laugh. Even when the gentlemen in town would come together, he'd tell us ridiculous stories. Local legends, mostly. Things about fairies and elves."

"They were lovely people," Mrs. Thornton added with a little sigh. "We will miss them. But we're so glad you are here now, Lady Felicity."

"Thank you. I'm not certain we can be as wonderful neighbors as they were," Felicity admitted with an apologetic glance around the table.

"Mrs. Deerwood wouldn't want you to compare yourself to them," Mr. Edwards said, a warm smile spreading across his face. "She never let people speak poorly of one another, or themselves."

"She would tell you to be your best self," Mrs. Moore said, a wistful expression curling her lips into a smile. "That was the advice she gave to me, when I arrived as a bride to the new vicar." She gave a fond glance to her husband. "She'd say, 'Be your best self, Eliza, and people will soon see how lucky they are to know you.'"

"We will always remember their kindness," Mrs. Thornton said.

"And Mrs. Deerwood's biscuits," Mrs. Edwards said with a teasing smile at her husband. "Isn't that right, darling?"

His cheeks pinked, and he raised his two hands almost defensively. "Her biscuits were the talk of the town. And even though it pains me to say it, I have never tasted anything as delicious in my life."

Reverend Moore, who had been listening intently, chimed in, "My wife and I only moved here two years ago, so we did not know them as well as some, but they always impressed me. Since their leaving, we've heard nothing but respect and admiration for the Deerwoods. Their legacy is will likely be felt in these parts for years to come. Biscuits notwithstanding."

Tad shared a rueful smile with Felicity. "It's a shame we

never had the chance to meet them, but their reputation certainly precedes them."

The conversation continued, weaving through different topics, but Felicity's mind kept returning to the Deerwoods. Their goodness still rippled through the community. It was a quality she admired and aspired to emulate.

She caught Tad observing her a moment later, his expression contemplative. When their gazes met, he gave her the barest wink. She bit her lip and glanced away to keep from giggling. Her husband was becoming something of a flirt. And she adored it.

When the meal concluded, the women retired to the drawing room, leaving the men to their port and cigars. Mrs. Moore led Felicity and the other ladies to a set of plush chairs, her eyes twinkling with excitement.

"Lady Felicity," she began, "You'll recall the Ladies Aid Society I mentioned when we first met? Mrs. Thornton and Mrs. Edwards are two of our society's most contributing members." The three women beamed with happiness. "Every Christmas we put together charity boxes for the less fortunate members of our community. We fill them with food, clothing, and small tokens of love and care. It's a tradition that brings us great joy."

Felicity's eyes widened, and her heart warmed at the thought. "That's wonderful! What a lovely way to help others."

Mrs. Thornton clasped her hands together, her tone sincere. "It's a small gesture, but it means the world to those who receive it."

"And this year," Mrs. Edwards chimed in, her eyes sparkling, "we would be honored if you would join us, Lady Felicity."

Felicity's heart leaped in her chest. "I would be delighted to participate. Thank you for including me."

The women spent the next quarter hour discussing the

details. Felicity felt a sense of belonging, a connection that went beyond mere social courtesy.

TAD SAVORED THE RICH WARMTH OF THE SCOTTISH whiskey, the smoky flavor dancing on his tongue. The men had gathered around the table, a relaxed camaraderie filling the room. Reverend Moore's eyes twinkled as he raised his glass, leaning back in his chair.

"So, Mr. Harcourt," he began, his voice genial, "you must tell us how you came to marry the lovely Lady Felicity Harcourt."

Tad's heart skipped a beat, his fingers tightening around his glass. How could he explain the arrangements, the negotiations, without revealing the transactional nature of their union? He glanced around the table, meeting the curious gazes of the other men.

"Well, Mr. Moore," he replied, choosing his words carefully, "it was a fortunate circumstance that brought us together. We were both looking for a partner who shared similar values and goals."

Mr. Edwards, the youthful romantic, grinned broadly. "Similar values and goals? Come off it man. You are besotted with each other. It's evident in the way you look at her."

Tad's cheeks warmed, the other man's observation touching a hidden longing within him.

Mr. Thornton, the older gentleman, scoffed at the idea, his voice dripping with condescension. "Marrying for love? Such a youthful folly. My wife and I married for mutual benefit, and we've been content all these years. These new romantic ideas are pure nonsense. An effect of too much novel reading, if you ask me."

The room filled with a spirited debate, the men's voices rising and falling as they exchanged opinions.

Mr. Thornton's stern face tightened as he said, "Romantic notions are for the young and foolish. A sensible marriage is built on mutual interests and respect. Love is a fleeting sentiment, but deep and abiding affection for one another grows over time."

Mr. Edwards, however, shook his head, his eyes glowing with passion. "Love is the very essence of life, Mr. Thornton. I cannot imagine a union without it. My wife and I found each other through it, and our love grows stronger every day. How can one dismiss such a powerful connection?"

Mr. Moore cleared his throat, drawing their attention. His gentle eyes met Tad's, as though sensing his inner turmoil. "Gentlemen, I believe love can grow in many circumstances. It doesn't always begin with the romance we find in novels; sometimes, it starts as a seed and blossoms over time. Like a garden, love requires nurturing, patience, and care. Even the most unlikely pair can find love if they tend to it diligently."

Tad's heart ached at the vicar's words. He wanted to believe in love's potential, in the possibility of something deep and rich growing between him and Felicity. But the doubts still nagged at him. They grew closer to one another, he enjoyed her companionship. She seemed to enjoy his too. But love?

Mr. Edwards smiled warmly at the vicar. "Well said, Mr. Moore. There is hope in love, and it transcends all differences."

Mr. Thornton merely grunted, unconvinced, swirling his whiskey. "Hope and love may warm the heart, but they don't put food on the table. Practicality has its merits."

Tad's mind wandered, his thoughts consumed by the topic at hand. The conversation around him seemed to mirror his inner conflict, the clashing opinions echoing his own uncertainty. He glanced towards the door, imagining Felicity laughing with the ladies, her face aglow with joy.

Could they find more than contentment between them? Could they overcome their differences and nurture the fragile bond that had begun to form?

The weight of the question settled heavily on his shoulders.

Were he and Felicity too different? They came from different worlds, different backgrounds, and their personalities were distinct. He was reserved, plainspoken, pragmatic, work-focused, while she was refined, graceful, and accustomed to a relaxed life he could never fully comprehend.

A fairy, an angel.

He looked down at his hands, the memories of his father's gruff demeanor toward his mother taunting him. He didn't want to become that. Oh, he knew his parents cared for each other. There was ample evidence of that in the way they supported one another. But his father always, always put the business first. His family second. His reputation was his top priority. His wife's heart less so. Tad wanted more for Felicity and himself. But was it possible?

The conversation continued around him, but for Tad, a seed of doubt had been planted, and he knew that only time would tell if their marriage could blossom into something beautiful.

For now, all he could do was hope and strive to be the husband his wife deserved.

He raised his glass, forcing a smile, toasting to the future when the other gentleman raised their own. But deep down, uncertainty kept its grip on him, and it couldn't be washed down with even the finest of Scottish whiskeys.

Eleven

A few days later, Tad sat near the fire in Felicity's favored sitting room. His wife stood near the window, hand on the glass. He watched as she gazed out, her eyes wide at the shimmering ice that had encased the world outside. The words of the vicar still echoed in his mind, a challenge he was ready to meet.

"Fancy a skate on the lawn?" he asked, joining her at the window. "We could slip and slide our way into becoming the most graceful skaters in the county."

She turned to him, a laugh escaping her lips. "Oh, I can just imagine the gossip in the local papers: 'Mr. Harcourt and His Graceless Wife tumble to their doom on the icy grounds of their estate.' It would cause a sensation, don't you think?"

His heart lightened at her humor. "A sensation I would most love to cause with you." He took her hand, leading her out of the quiet chamber and towards the ballroom. "But we must prepare for our grand event. I've decided today is a day for us, my dear. A day to explore our new home and make plans."

A soft blush tinged her cheeks, but her eyes sparkled with curiosity. "I would enjoy that, Tad."

They entered the ballroom, its grandeur still awaiting a festive touch. Felicity's eyes danced over the chandeliers, the polished floor, the tall windows.

"What do you envision?" Tad asked, intrigued by her thoughts. "It's your canvas, my lady. Paint me a picture."

She walked through the room, her fingers trailing over the furniture. "I see candles, and greenery, and twinkling lights. I hear laughter and music. But most of all, I see people enjoying themselves, feeling welcome and cared for."

He followed her to the center of the room, his growing admiration warming him from head to toe. "Your heart is as grand as this room, Felicity. But tell me, where shall we place the mistletoe?"

Her eyes widened, and she stumbled over her words. "The m-mistletoe?"

Tad's grin widened, and he stepped closer. "Why, yes. It's a tradition, is it not? A kiss beneath the mistletoe?"

"It is more common below stairs," she informed him with a slight wrinkle above her nose. "Not at a formal event."

"Pity." He looked about with feigned disappointment. "No mistletoe, then?"

"Well." She drew the single word out and then sighed. "I suppose, as you are the master of the house, if you request mistletoe then I ought to find a place for it."

He picked up her hand in his, and the quick flood of pink into her cheeks gratified him entirely too much. "I would like that. You can tuck it away, if you wish. Only telling me where it is. Or do you fear my intentions?"

The teasing twinkle returned to her eyes. "Oh, I know your

intentions well enough, Mr. Harcourt. The question is, can you handle the consequences of following through?"

They laughed, their shared joy echoing in the room. The ice outside had imprisoned them, but within the walls of their house, where they were safe and warm, Tad couldn't be more content.

As the afternoon wore on, Tad and Felicity found themselves sitting by the fire in the ballroom, mugs of spiced tea in hand, the grand hall dimly lit yet glowing with the potential of their shared dreams.

"Felicity," Tad said as the conversation turned more personal, his voice gentle, "what was your favorite Christmas? Surely you've had many grand celebrations, as a noblewoman."

She looked into the fire, her eyes going distant, a smile playing on her lips. "Actually, there is one Christmas I remember most fondly. I was only six years old, and my parents were still alive."

Tad leaned forward, captivated by her voice, the emotion in her eyes. "Tell me about it."

She chuckled, a touch of sadness in her eyes. "Oh, it was marvelous. They gave me a beautiful kitten, soft and striped with amber eyes, and an intricately crafted dollhouse. I ended up turning the dollhouse into the kitten's home. You should have seen the mess it made of the tiny furniture!"

He laughed with her, imagining the scene, but he saw something deeper in her eyes, a longing perhaps. "That sounds like a wonderful memory."

Her face softened, the laughter fading. "Yes, it was. They died the following spring, you see, taken by illness."

He reached out, covering her hand with his, her skin cool beneath his touch. "I'm sorry, Felicity."

She looked at him, her eyes filled with a quiet sadness. "I

wish I remembered them more. But that Christmas, those precious memories, they keep them alive for me."

He squeezed her hand, understanding her loss. "What happened to the kitten?"

Her smile turned wistful. "I had to give her up when I went to live with my grandmother in the dower house. My grandmother would sneeze terribly whenever a cat was near."

He saw a hint of a tear in her eye, and he realized how much she had lost, how much she had endured. As a child, she would have drawn much-needed comfort from the gifted pet. "You've been strong, Felicity. And you've grown to be such a compassionate person, despite your losses. Or perhaps because of them."

She met his gaze, her smile returning, softer now. "I try, as many do. And now I have a new beginning with you."

They sat there, the fire crackling, their hands entwined, the past and the future merging in a single moment. Tad knew then that he would do anything, give anything, to make this woman happy, to be the joy in her life that she had once found in a playful kitten and a loving family.

Felicity's hand squeezed his, a look of curiosity in her eyes. "What about you, Tad? What was your favorite Christmas?"

He looked away for a moment, the warmth of the fire suddenly feeling distant. He should've expected her question.

"Truth be told," he began slowly, "I cannot remember a time when my family celebrated Christmas together. Father was always consumed with work, saying we hadn't the money or time to waste. Mother didn't wish to go against his word. Before I knew it, I found myself swept into the business as well."

Her face fell, a look of sympathy in her eyes. "I'm sorry. That must have been lonely."

He shrugged, trying to brush off the sting of the memories.

"It was what it was. We had our successes, our triumphs. They were our family celebrations."

She looked at him, her eyes searching his, as if trying to reach deeper. "But surely you must have wished for something more. Something personal, something joyful?"

He looked into her eyes, the depths of green and gold drawing him in. Suddenly, the emptiness of those past Christmases seemed more pronounced, the longing for something more, something real, more acute.

"I suppose I did," he admitted, his voice barely above a whisper. "I suppose I always wished for something more."

She raised her hand, her fingers gently brushing his cheek. "We ought to make this Christmas something special. Something just for us."

He smiled, the weight of the past lifting. "This first Christmas with you will certainly be my favorite."

Her eyes sparkled, her smile radiant. "I hope so."

He pulled her closer, wrapping his arms around her. They fell silent, watching the flames. Saying nothing more of the past.

Twelve

DECEMBER 12TH

Felicity watched as Tad's brow furrowed, his attention on the documents spread across his desk. She knew that the work of running an estate could be demanding. Many gentlemen employed stewards and secretaries to handle everything, but Tad wanted a working knowledge of his new holdings. She admired that aspect of his character. He never seemed to like sitting still unless he had a problem to solve or calculations to make.

Or unless he was with her, by the fire. Then he seemed content to do nothing.

"Would you like to know what this is about?" he asked suddenly, catching her gaze.

Her heart leapt with surprise. "Truly? You wouldn't mind explaining it to me?"

His eyebrows drew together, as though perplexed by her question. "Of course. Everything about the management of our estate affects you too. You ought to know the intricacies of it. If you wish. Besides, I may need help from time to time with making decisions. And I trust your judgment."

He did?

She came to stand beside his chair, but Tad hastily stood and gestured for her to sit. Once she had, he leaned closer to point to the document he'd been studying. "This is one of the agreements we have with a tenant. It looks as though the Deerwoods first leased a farm to the current holder's father, thirty years ago. The son took over payment and management on the thirty year lease only four years ago. The lease comes to an end next month."

"Does he want to renew it?" she asked, studying the dates and the agreement.

"He does. So, I asked the land steward for the records of payment." He pulled a book from the corner of the desk closer and pointed to a row of columns with dates and numbers. "His father never missed a single payment. They were always on time, and always in full. And the son was equally as dutiful. But here, you can see he hasn't made his last two payments."

"Why would he do so well and then fall behind?"

"I asked the same thing. The steward obtained a letter from the farmer, Mr. Arnold. Here it is." He lifted the lease to show her the letter beneath it, written in pencil rather than ink. "Read it and tell me what you think."

She read the letter aloud.

Mr. Harcourt,

I hope this letter finds you in good health. I write to you requesting your patience and grace in a most regrettable matter. I must address the matter of my failure to meet the lease payments for these last two months.

My late father, a man of unwavering integrity, never missed a payment for the farm he cherished. It is a tradition I have proudly upheld until now. The farm has been our family's heart and home, and I am committed to preserving it for my children, as my father did for me.

However, recent events have conspired against me. My wife gave birth to our fifth child, and both mother and child were gravely ill. The cost of hiring a wet nurse and doctor were dear. The need to care for them has left my eldest son and me in difficult times, hindering our efforts to bring in the harvest.

Then our only plow horse went lame, delaying our crops' journey to market. By the time we managed, the demand had fallen, and we made less than usual.

I assure you, sir, that my intentions are honorable, and my commitment to our agreement remains unshaken. I beg for your patience and understanding. I am determined to settle the debt, but I must ask for more time.

Would it be possible for us to meet in person? I wish to explain my situation more fully and discuss any means by which I might satisfy my obligations while preserving the only home my family has ever known.

I await your reply and remain,

Your servant, John Arnold

"Oh, the poor man. His poor family." She covered her heart with her hand as she imagined the difficulty they had faced. The frustration and worry the husband must feel for his wife, child, and his home. She looked up at her husband to find him watching her, his brow furrowed. "What will you do, Tad?"

"What do you think we ought to do?" he asked, his tone soft and eyes inviting.

"We?" she repeated, laying the letter down on the desk. He only nodded, staring at her. Waiting for her answer. She cleared her throat and looked at the ledger again, where numbers told nothing of the man's story. Only of payments made. Surely the money was of top priority to Tad. "Can we afford a delay in his rents?"

Tad's eyebrows raised. "We can, in fact. Mr. Deerwood set

aside a percentage of every payment made by all tenants into a fund. Here." Tad slid another book closer to her and tapped the page. "This fund is only drawn from to make repairs to roads, buildings, and the things the estate holder is responsible for maintaining. It's a large sum. But even without access to it, the rents paid on other properties cover the costs of taxes and running the estate. And, of course, I still hold stock in my father's shipping company. Mr. Arnold's lack of payment hasn't harmed us in the slightest."

Felicity chewed her bottom lip, her heart whispering what should be done. But would Tad, a merchant in breeding, feel as she did?

His deep brown gaze stayed upon her, coaxing her as gently as his words did. "Tell me your thoughts, my Felicity."

"His letter seems most desperate," she said, lifting the sheet again. "So many women are lost in childbirth. So many infants never have the chance to take their first steps. His heart must be broken, his spirits low. I cannot imagine the anxieties he would face, and the fear of being turned out of his house? He doesn't even know you, Tad. He doesn't know if you're compassionate or a man driven by greed."

He husband nodded along, but said nothing.

What was the worst that could happen, if she spoke her idea out loud? He might laugh at her. Dismiss it. Explain why such a thing wasn't practical or possible. And she would be disappointed—in him, rather than in herself.

She took in a fortifying breath, then picked up her husband's hand. "I think you—we, I mean. I think *we* should forgive him the two months' rent, and perhaps find a way to help his family. Winter is coming, and they must be so worried about further illness."

His brows relaxed, all tension gone from around his eyes, and his lips curved into the faintest of smiles. "I agree with you."

Such simple words, and yet they filled her with incredible relief. Joy. And even pride in her husband. "You do? Truly?"

He nodded. "I thought I could visit Mr. Arnold tomorrow, perhaps. With a new lease for him to sign. I want to be certain he's honest, and I think I will have a better understanding if I meet him in person. But if he's sincere, I thought forgiving the debt would be best."

"Because it is the kind thing to do?" she asked with eagerness.

"Yes." He squeezed her hand clasped in his. "But if it makes you feel better, as I can see your heart is quite hardened—" He grinned as he teased her. "It would also make sense to keep on a tenant who loves his farm. Mr. Arnold grew up there. He knows the people in the community, he attends the same church we do. He wants to be here, in this place. Turning him out to bring in a stranger, whose character we wouldn't know, whose history might not be so connected, would be a risk."

Felicity leaned closer to her husband. "Showing a tenant such as Mr. Arnold compassion will also build good will with our neighbors."

"There. You have the heart of a money-grabbing merchant."

She laughed and shook her head at him. "I think you're using all this fine business sense of yours as justification to do what you want."

"Really? What is it I want?"

Her heart softened and she laid her hand against his cheek. "To be kind to someone who is in need."

Tad covered her hand and turned to kiss the inside of her palm, making her pulse race and her stomach twist in a decidedly pleasant way. "You mustn't tell anyone I think of things other than ledgers and bank accounts."

"Not a soul," she promised, but she wouldn't need to tell anyone. It wouldn't be long before their new friends and neighbors saw the sort of man she'd married. A man so thoughtful of others it made her heart ache with happiness.

"Now that we have that matter sorted. Let's look at another piece of business." He stood to his full height again and shifted papers around, presenting her with a new situation. One involving the purchase of more sheep.

As he explained the intricacies of his work, Felicity listened attentively, her mind whirring with ideas.

He met each of her suggestions with consideration, and she found herself growing more confident, more a part of his life. The morning passed in a mix of business and household conversation.

The snow-covered gardens beckoned them after lunch, and they ventured out, wrapped in warm coats and scarves. Felicity's laughter rang through the crisp air as Tad took her hand, leading her down a path he claimed to have never explored.

"Look at this lovely place," she exclaimed, her eyes wide with wonder as they stumbled upon a hidden alcove, framed by ancient trees and sheltered by a snow-draped trellis.

"It's like something out of a fairy tale," Tad murmured, his voice tinged with awe.

Felicity turned to him, admiring the wonder in his eyes. This could be a special place, a sanctuary for their growing relationship. Every day that passed, she saw the possibility of weaving joy and love into the fabric of their marriage.

"We should come here often," she said softly, squeezing his hand.

He nodded, a smile playing on his lips. "I'd like that very much."

The cold meant they didn't stay out long. When they returned indoors, they settled on the sofa in his study. She took out her notebook, where she'd been recording her plans and thoughts for the ball.

She asked for his opinion on everything, and he refused to answer her seriously.

"You can't possibly want haggis for the midnight supper!" She laughed, nudging him playfully with her shoulder.

"It's a fine Scottish dish," he defended, pretended offense in his tone.

"Neither of us are Scottish." She poked him in the side with her finger, and he arched away from her.

"Must one be Scottish to enjoy haggis?"

"Yes." She glowered at him. "Because it's obviously a taste one must be born to, as I cannot believe such a thing could be acquired, no matter how much one tries."

They bantered and teased, planning the menu, selecting the music, and envisioning the dances. Each decision was a step closer to creating a celebration both for their guests and for themselves.

The evening wore on, and Felicity found herself lost in the joy of the moment, grateful for Tad's presence and hopeful for their future. Her heart was set on a path, one that would guide them both to a life filled with love, understanding, and the simple joys she so dearly wished to share with him.

The plans for the ball were more than a celebration; they were a symbol of their partnership, a dance of hopes and dreams. And as the embers in the fireplace glowed, Felicity knew that they were on their way to something beautiful, something uniquely theirs. She could feel it.

Thirteen

DECEMBER 17TH

As the sleigh's runners cut through the pristine snow, Felicity felt a surge of pure, unbridled joy. Last night's snowfall had transformed the world into a spectacle of white, every tree branch and fence post adorned with a delicate frosting of white. The countryside spread before them in an endless expanse of shimmering tranquility, untouched and pure.

Mrs. Moore, Mrs. Edwards, and Mrs. Thornton kept their faces untucked from their scarves, as thrilled with the outing as Felicity herself. The cold air kissed their cheeks and brought an invigorating, delightful sting. Their breath misted before them and soon joined the snowflakes that danced and twirled in the wake of the sleigh.

Against the frozen earth, the horses' hooves thumped a cheerful rhythm. Mrs. Thornton drove the team, proving an expert with the reins.

"This is wonderful," Felicity said from her place on the second seat. But the woosh of the cold wind carried her voice away.

"What, dear?" Mrs. Moore shouted.

"This is wonderful!" Felicity shouted back, then laughed at how silly it felt of her to attempt a conversation in such circumstances.

"Oh yes! Nothing is better than a sleigh ride through the snow," Mrs. Moore agreed loudly.

With a hand to her fur-lined cap, Mrs. Edwards turned to face them from her place beside their driver. "Far better than the gray slush of London's streets, isn't it?"

Together, they flew across the snow, laughing and shouting to one another. The chill of the air, the beauty of the landscape, and the thrill of motion combined to create a memory that Felicity would hold dear for years to come. She felt certain of it.

The sleigh slowed as it approached a row of tenant houses, their modest structures nestled together, smoke rising from chimneys and the soft glow of hearth fires visible through the windows.

As the sleigh glided to a stop, Felicity felt a pang of longing, a wish that the ride could last forever, but also a profound gratitude for the experience, for the memory, and for the shared connection that had deepened among her new friends.

"Now, on to work," Mrs. Moore said, grinning at them as she slid the robe from her lap. "There is much to do."

The women disembarked, Felicity's heart swelling with anticipation and purpose. The sparkle in the eyes of Mrs. Moore, Mrs. Edwards, and Mrs. Thornton mirrored her own excitement, a shared commitment to a mission of compassion and care.

"It's Lady Felicity," a little girl shouted as she darted out the door and into the snow. "Do you remember me, Lady?"

"Of course I do." Felicity plucked a large gingerbread biscuit from the basket in her arms and held it out to the little girl. "You're Ellen. We built the snowmen together."

Ellen giggled as she accepted the biscuit, and her mother

came out with a hand on her rounded middle. "Mind you say thank you, Ellie girl."

"Thank you, Lady." Ellen curtsied. "Is there a biscuit for my mum?"

"There are biscuits and blankets, pies, and warm mittens for everyone," Mrs. Edwards said.

A crowd of children staring from the next house cheered, and Mrs. Thornton went toward them with a cheery grin. "Look at all you find lads. Harry, Jack, and Edward, help us get the winter gifts from the sleigh."

As they moved from house to house, they were greeted with smiling faces, and eyes brightening with joy. The children's laughter rang like music, pure and sweet, as they darted around their mothers, their curious eyes taking in the boxes filled with provisions.

Then the ladies returned to their sleigh and were off again, to another cottage where four generations of women lived together while their menfolk had gone to London in search of work.

Felicity's care and love for her new home, and the people surrounding it, deepened. She was not just the lady of Winterway House; she was a friend, a neighbor, someone who listened as women spoke of babies on the way and as grand-mothers clucked their tongues and offered sage advice on keeping well in cold weather.

Yet, as the day wore on, a slight headache nagged at her temples, an insistent throb that seemed to pulse in time with the horses' hooves against the snow. A series of sneezes escaped her lips, each one a jarring interruption to the joy she was feeling.

"Oh, my dear. Are you all right?" Mrs. Edwards asked with a wince after an especially unladylike, eruptive sneeze.

"Merely a slight tickle in my nose, from the cold air." She brushed the concern aside with a graceful wave of her handkerchief, unwilling to let anything dampen her spirits or distract from the importance of the task at hand. "I'm quite all right. Do, let's continue. Tell me more about Mr. and Mrs. Farrow."

Despite her attempts to ignore it, the discomfort lingered. Her body's protests of the cold and exertion most inconvenient.

"Lady Felicity, you've turned quite pale." Mrs. Moore peered at her after another lovely visit with an elderly couple.

Felicity used her most reassuring tone. "It is nothing a little tea will not put to rights again."

"One last house," Mrs. Thornton declared. "And then we will take you home. A chill can quickly become something more serious, if not tended to."

Though she wanted to protest, another sneeze wracked Felicity's body, making her chest ache. "Very well. Thank you."

"What sort of friends would we be if we let you grow ill?" Mrs. Moore asked.

Mrs. Edwards grinned with a touch of mischief. "And we cannot have you calling off the winter ball because of a little cold, now, can we?"

They all laughed, and Felicity settled deeper into the fur robes.

Upon arriving home, she was greeted in the entryway by Tad's warm smile, his eyes lighting up as he took in her flushed cheeks and sparkling eyes. As though he was eager to be with her again, perhaps even watching for her arrival from an upstairs window. He brushed the footman aside and helped her remove her coat, hat, and gloves. Then he cupped her cheek in one hand, his thumb brushing gently against her skin.

"You look radiant. Like a winter fairy." He spoke in a voice filled with admiration and a hint of curiosity. "But you also look tired. Was the day taxing?"

She shook her head, her smile undimmed, even as the fatigue

settled into her bones. "It was wonderful, Tad. Truly wonderful. The people, the children . . . My heart has never been so full." Her voice trailed off, a contented sigh escaping her lips as she leaned into his touch, the warmth of his hand a comfort to her chilled skin.

He studied her for a moment, his eyes searching. He finally nodded, accepting her words as he tucked a stray lock of hair behind her ear. "Come rest by the fire, Felicity. You've earned it."

Her heart swelled at his understanding, his gentle concern. She allowed him to lead her to their favorite sofa in the upstairs sitting room, knowing that the comfort of their home and Tad's attentive care would soon ease the minor ailments of the day.

"What was your favorite part of the day?" He bent to stoke the fire in the room.

"May I say 'everything?'" Felicity laughed, though the air caught in her airway sharply. She cleared her throat. "I saw all the little ones who helped you build the snowmen in the village."

He ordered tea, then settled next to her and asked more questions abouts her day. He laughed when she told him of how happy the biscuits made the children. He feigned disappointment when she informed him no one declared the biscuits as good as Mrs. Deerwood's had been. When the tea arrived, Felicity rose without thought to pour out for them both.

She stumbled slightly as a sudden wave of fatigue washed over her, and Tad's smile turned to a look of concern.

"Felicity? Is something wrong?"

"I am quite well." She winced when he raised his eyebrows at her, the doubt clear on his face. "I suppose I have a small headache." Then she shivered.

"You're not well," he said, his voice soft but firm. He rose from the sofa. "You need to rest."

"I'm fine, merely tired," she protested, but the sneeze that followed betrayed her.

Tad's face set in a gentle but unyielding expression. "To bed, my love. You need to take care of yourself."

Before she could react to this new form of address, a cough tore up her throat, and she barely had enough warning to turn from her husband and raise her wrist to cover her mouth.

The moment she recovered, Felicity found herself being guided to her bedroom, the tender concern in Tad's eyes melting what remained of her resistance. He rang for Clara, but Tad didn't hesitate to make her sit on the edge of her bed. He removed her shoes, and her snow-dampened stockings. She couldn't form any words of protest. And why would she need to? He had spent nights in the bed beside her, both of them in night-clothes. Their bare feet had touched more than once. And she'd woken in the night to find his arm draped over her waist.

She gave him a confused look, having to turn her head to peer over her shoulder at him. He knelt on the bed behind her to undo the buttons of her dress, his eyebrows pulled tightly together in concentration.

"Why do you sleep in here every night?" she asked. "Is my bed more comfortable than yours?"

"Something like that," he muttered.

She'd never dared ask him before. Just as she'd never dared ask when—or if—he intended to consummate their marriage. He'd shown a great deal of affection in other ways. Perhaps she had been mistaken about the timing of such things.

"I will ask Mrs. Moore about it," she said aloud.

"What will you ask the vicar's wife?" her husband asked, helping her slide the dress over her shoulders and leaving her in her underthings.

"Wifely things." She dismissed the topic with a wave of her

hand, then winced and put the same hand to her temple. "I detest catching cold."

"Most people do." He kissed her temple. A knock at the door heralded Clara's arrival, and Tad stepped away to address the maid. "She has a headache and hasn't had her tea yet. I'll have something sent up for her. Please, make her as warm and comfortable as you can."

"Of course, sir," Clara answered. Then she helped Felicity in and out of more layers before putting a warm brick at the bottom of the bed and tucking the blankets around her mistress's shoulders. Tad had left, at some point. But the tea arrived.

"I wish he'd stayed," Felicity muttered before sipping at the tea, bitter with herbs meant to soothe her head and throat. "Tad keeps me warmer than the quilt will."

Clara giggled for some reason. "I'm certain that's true, my lady. But Mr. Harcourt wants you to get your rest. He has other things to see to. So the quilt must do for now."

"Very well." Felicity let her bottom lip protrude in the manner her grandmother had insisted wasn't right for a young lady to allow. "You must tell him I miss him, though."

As she settled into bed, wrapped in warmth and comfort, she fell into a doze. And then a nap. And before she knew it, her eyes opened, and it was dark. A familiar form bent over her.

"Sleep well, my love."

It was Tad. And there was that wonderful, frightening endearment again. If only she didn't feel so heavy, all over, she might have asked him about it. Instead, she managed a sigh of contentment.

And as she drifted into sleep, the memory of Tad's soft kiss on her forehead, she danced into a dream of snowflakes and mistletoe.

※

TAD PACED THE FLOOR OF HIS STUDY, WORRY GNAWING AT his insides. Felicity's sneezing and headache had turned overnight into something more concerning, and he couldn't shake the feeling that he needed to do something, anything, to help her.

With a determined stride, he made his way to find Mrs. Bennet, the housekeeper. Below stairs, where the staff never welcomed their master or mistress. It was their domain, but he trespassed without the slightest hesitation. The housekeeper's years of wisdom and knowledge of the local area would surely guide him.

"Mrs. Bennet," he said, his voice tinged with urgency. "I'm worried about Lady Felicity. I believe we should send for a physician."

Mrs. Bennet's eyes met his. She glanced at the maid she'd been speaking to, giving a nod of dismissal. Then she came to Tad, where he stood in the doorway to the corridor. "I understand your concern, sir, but there is no physician nearby. The nearest one is in the next village, and it would take hours to fetch him. However, the apothecary in the Hollow may have something to help. He's a knowledgeable man and has aided us many times before."

Tad's brow furrowed, torn between the desire for immediate action and trusting the housekeeper.

"Has she a fever?" Mrs. Bennet folded her hands before her, appearing calm.

Tad shook her head. "No."

"Then an apothecary's tinctures and remedies will likely be enough to set her rights."

"Very well," he agreed, though the worry didn't leave him.

"Send someone to fetch what the apothecary recommends. Please." His hands clenched and unclenched at his sides.

Felicity didn't have a fever. He'd checked himself, a quarter hour ago. But she still shivered and sniffled. Said her head still hurt. Said nonsense things about decorating the ballroom in snowflakes and mistletoe.

Mrs. Bennet's hand reached out to touch his arm, her expression softening. "She will be fine, sir. I have seen many a cold come and go. The best medicine will be rest and the care you show."

With a nod, Tad left the servants' domain and made his way to Felicity's room, his heart heavy with concern. As he entered, he saw her resting, her face pale and dark circles beneath her eyes. Gently, he lowered himself to sit on the mattress beside her. He touched her forehead, finding it still cool. He released a sigh of relief.

Perhaps she wasn't so very ill.

Felicity's eyes fluttered open, a teasing smile playing on her lips. "My handsome nursemaid," she murmured, her voice weak but filled with affection.

He couldn't help but smile, the playful words a welcome relief from his worry. "I do my best, my lady. Though I fear I'm quite out of my depth."

She laughed softly, but her expression sobered as she took in his worried eyes. "Oh, Tad. I will be fine. It's a simple cold. I promise."

"I can't help but worry," he admitted, his voice catching.

Her hand caught his above the blankets. "Did I say strange things to you last evening?"

He looked at her delicate fingers, so small and fragile compared to his. "Somewhat strange. Yes. And this morning."

She winced. "I always do, when I'm ill. My grandmother's

physician said it was one of the strangest things he'd ever seen. I would babble everything in my head aloud."

"Ah. A perfect time to learn your secrets, then."

She narrowed her eyes at him. "Thankfully, I am quite myself now."

"Thankfully," he repeated with a smirk. Then he gave her hand another squeeze. "Perhaps I will stay here today. All day. In case you slip into such a state again."

"I haven't any secrets worth knowing, husband."

"Any secret of yours, large or small, I want to know." He cleared his throat when her eyes widened and stepped away from the bed. "And that isn't the only reason to remain here. I've learned we haven't a doctor nearby. That leaves it to me to see to your recovery."

She managed a playful look. "Who will read poetry to me if you're too busy playing doctor?"

"Who will read poetry to *me* if you are ill?" he countered, relieved to see the gleam of interest in her eyes. "I might have to resort to reading dull letters of business."

"Oh, how horrible for you," she exclaimed, one hand to her chest as she feigned dismay.

"Desperate times call for desperate measures." He kept the words light, but something of his concern must've shown in his expression.

His wife reached for his hand again, and he gave it to her. Uncertain why, when she was ill, he was the one who needed comforting.

"You worry too much. I'll be well again in no time, pestering you with verses and rhymes."

"I shall hold you to that, my lady," he said, squeezing her hand. She gave his hand a tug and he sat next to her again, sliding off his shoes and sitting alongside her. Felicity rested her head against his chest.

They sat together, their gentle teasing turning to comfortable silence.

Tad's worry persisted, a constant presence. He kissed the top of her head, and he trusted she would be well again soon. He doubted he would rest much in the meantime.

Fourteen

DECEMBER 19TH

The grand ballroom of Winterway House was a flurry of activity. Felicity stood in the center of the room, surrounded by servants carrying garlands, silver baubles, and candles. The rich scent of pine and the buzz of anticipation filled the air.

Despite her recent illness, she felt beautifully alive, a part of something vibrant and joyful. The ball was only three days away, and everything had to be perfect.

"Tighter, there, on the left side," she instructed, pointing to a garland. "And more candles by the windows. We want the room to gleam."

"Yes, Lady Felicity," the head footman replied, bowing slightly before scurrying off to follow her directions.

A gentle touch on her arm made her turn, and she found herself face to face with Tad. His eyes were dark with concern, his brow slightly furrowed.

"Felicity, you should be resting," he said, his voice gentle. "You've only just recovered, and I worry that you're overexerting yourself."

She shook her head and gave him a reassuring pat on his hand. "I feel perfectly well, Tad. Truly, I do. And this," she gestured to the bustling room, "is invigorating."

"Are you certain?"

"Very." His worry for her made her heart grow warm, along with the rest of her. No one cared for her the way Tad did. He'd stayed near during her two days of illness, plying her with remedy-filled tea and books of poetry. Then allowing her to use him for a pillow when she napped. It was almost a shame to be well again.

He regarded her for a long moment, his eyes searching hers. Then he reached into his pocket and pulled out a small sprig of mistletoe wrapped in a delicate silver ribbon.

"For you," he said, placing it in her hand. "I thought you might find a special place for it."

Felicity's cheeks warmed this time, and she looked up at him with dismay. "Did you fetch this yourself?"

His grin of self-satisfaction was answer enough, but he shrugged and said, "I told you I wanted mistletoe somewhere. Just for the two of us."

"So you expect me to put it where you might find it most conveniently."

"That would be ideal, yes." He didn't have any shame, her handsome husband.

She tucked the mistletoe into her bodice, glowering at him. "I refuse to make it too easy for you."

His eyes twinkled, and he leaned in, his voice low. "I shall look forward to discovering its location then."

They stood together, the room around them alive with activity, yet for that moment, it was as if they were the only two people in the world.

The connection between them had grown, their shared experiences and playful banter deepening into something more profound. Neither had spoken the words, but the feelings were there, a glowing ember waiting to be fanned into flame.

With a gentle touch to her hand and a promise in his eyes, Tad left her to continue her work, his gift remained with her.

Felicity watched as Tad left the ballroom, his tall figure disappearing through the doorway. The mistletoe pressing against her skin seemed to pulse with the rhythm of her heart.

They had shared so much in their weeks together—laughter, understanding, and an intimacy that went beyond mere friendship. Yet, a nagging worry persisted in her mind. Was Tad's kindness and attention merely the dutiful actions of a good husband? Or was he, like her, quietly falling in love?

She sighed and turned back to the decorations. The question hovered in the back of her mind, sweet and tantalizing, filling her with both hope and uncertainty. As she worked, she found herself glancing toward the doorway where Tad had left. Yet the afternoon continued, the ballroom transforming under her watchful eye. The chandeliers sparkled, the garlands draped elegantly, and the room took on a festive charm.

Her mind, however, remained restless, her thoughts always circling back to Tad. The memory of his touch, the concern in his voice when she was ill, the way he'd held her hand as if it were the most natural thing in the world. His affection felt real, but was it enough? It all felt like love, but she couldn't be sure.

As evening approached, Tad reappeared, his eyes immediately seeking her out. She watched as he spoke with the servants, his manner easy and confident, but his gaze kept returning to her, a question in his eyes.

He approached her, a smile playing on his lips. "You've outdone yourself, Felicity. The room looks magnificent."

"Thank you, Tad," she replied, her voice slightly breathless.

"And what of my mistletoe?" He asked, glancing about as though hoping to find it right that moment.

She pulled out the mistletoe, holding it up between them. "Patience, Tad. I haven't decided where to put it yet."

His fingers brushed hers as he took the sprig. "Shall I hang it myself?" The question was a whisper in the growing darkness. "In a place only we shall know?"

The words sent a thrill through her, and she looked up at him, a question on the tip of her tongue. Did he feel as she did? Was this the moment he confessed it? Would he finally say the words she longed to hear?

"I—I—might know where to place it." Her stuttered answer only served to make him smile wider, and he returned the mistletoe to her.

His gaze warm but guarded, and offered her his arm. "Dinner is already on the table. I think we will forgo dressing for the meal tonight. You must be quite hungry after all your work."

"Yes," she agreed, forcing a smile. "I could eat an entire goose."

He laughed. "We're saving the goose for Christmas, otherwise, I would let you have it."

The room was ready, the decorations perfect. But Felicity's heart remained waiting, expectantly, for more. Tad was everything she'd hoped for and more, yet the question remained—was he in love with her? Or was she merely seeing what she wanted to see?

As she walked with him to the dining room, her thoughts were a whirl, the image of Tad and the sprig of mistletoe intertwining with her dreams and fears. She wanted to believe in love, but uncertainty remained, leaving her both joyful and restless as she waited.

Fifteen

Tad stood in the doorway between his room and Felicity's, the knob of the open door in hand. The only sound in the room was her soft breathing. As he leaned into her domain, his gaze turned to Felicity where she lay curled up in her blankets. Warm. Soft. Beautiful.

He thought of her every moment they were apart, remembering everything about their time together. The way her laughter filled the rooms of their new home, the way her eyes sparkled when she was deep in thought, and the way her presence had come to mean everything to him.

He didn't move from that place, from the doorway that separated his chamber from hers. He had slept alone in his room since her illness. Given his overabundance of caution. He was beginning to feel the weight of his decision, leaving matters unsaid, waiting for some unknown signal to proceed in the natural way of things.

Desire was not a stranger to him; he felt the longing, the pull towards her with an intensity that both thrilled and frightened him. But what he felt for Felicity was more than mere attraction.

He was falling in love, and the realization filled him with a mixture of joy and trepidation.

He quietly entered the room, his movements heavy with thought. He dropped a kiss on his wife's forehead, relieved to find it cool. He'd never known real fear until she grew ill. And it had only been a cold! But the possibility of it becoming more, of his wife falling seriously ill . . . It had been much to bare.

He returned to his own room, closing the door softly behind him. He dressed quickly, his mind still on Felicity, on the uncertainty that marked their relationship. He wanted her, needed her, not just as his wife but as the woman he loved. But he couldn't give in to his desires, not when he still had doubts about how to proceed, and about whether her feelings matched his.

His days had been filled with learning the intricacies of being a gentleman and a landowner. It was a world far removed from running his family business, a world filled with traditions and responsibilities he was only beginning to understand.

He was determined to excel, to prove to himself and to Felicity that he belonged in this world she was born into. But he feared that he would never be enough, that he would somehow fail her.

As he made his way out of his room to the empty corridor, he cast one last longing glance at the door that divided them. It was a barrier, symbolizing all that yet held him back. Barriers he was desperate to raze to the ground.

He shook his head, forcing himself to focus on the day ahead. He had much to learn, much to prove, and he couldn't allow his doubts to hold him back.

As he sat down to his breakfast, his thoughts once again turned to his wife. Would she hide the mistletoe, or neglect it entirely? He hadn't sensed any eagerness to attend to the task, nor to let him see to it. He hoped he had only caught her off guard.

He finished his meal in silence, his mind a whirl of emotions. He was on the brink of something beautiful, something profound, but he couldn't shake the fear that he might lose it all. He needed to find the courage to take the next step, to bridge the gap between them, and to finally allow himself to love and be loved in return.

With a determined set to his jaw, he rose from the table, his mind made up. He would talk to Felicity, he would find a way to express what he felt. The time had come to face his fears and embrace the love that he felt blossoming between them.

The night of the ball would be the perfect time to tell her everything in his heart. At the height of her triumph, after a night of laughter, celebration, and dancing. It would be an unforgettable moment. A culmination of their working together to build a new life at Winterway House.

He knew it wouldn't be easy, but he was ready. For Felicity, for love, he would risk his heart.

Sixteen

DECEMBER 21ST

The night of the ball had arrived, and Felicity scarcely contained her excitement. The grand ballroom of Winterway House was aglow with candles and shimmering chandeliers, the floors polished to a gleaming finish, and the room filled with the intoxicating scent of pine and mint.

Guests were arriving, elegant and cheerful, their compliments and laughter filling the air as the musicians began to pluck at their instruments. Felicity stood alongside Tad, her heart swelling with pride as they greeted their friends and neighbors. Everything was perfect, exactly as she'd hoped, and she could see the happiness in Tad's eyes as well.

Lady Victoria Wainwright swept into the receiving line, her nose in the air and her disdain for all things common clear in her eyes. "What a pretty job you've done on this room, my dear," the woman said without real warmth. "It reminds me of a private party I attended in London last Season."

Nothing Lady Victoria said could truly upset Felicity's inner serenity. Though they were equal in status, both granddaughters and daughters of earls, they barely knew one another and had almost nothing in common. Had there been any other entertainment for Lady Victoria to pursue that evening, Felicity highly doubted she would have attended.

"I quite like how everything turned out," Felicity said, glancing up at the glittering chandeliers. "It was good of you to come. Is your husband with you?"

Tad was conversing with another guest, seemingly not paying any attention to Lady Victoria's arrival.

"No. He thinks such things a waste of his time." Lady Victoria wrinkled her nose and wafted a hand in front of her as though to wave away the thought of her husband. "My cousin was sweet to accompany me, though. You know him, of course."

It took Felicity a moment to recall the family tree of her guest, but she realized the identity of Lady Victoria's companion at the same instant he came through the door, adjusting the points of his shirt.

"Lord William," she said aloud at the same time as Lady Victoria.

His easy smile and twinkling eyes were as friendly as ever when he approached, a hand outstretched to take hers. She gave it to him without hesitation.

"Goodness. What are you doing here?" She blurted the question quite accidentally as he took her hand and bowed over it with exaggerated gallantry.

"My dear Lady Felicity," he replied, his voice dripping with charm, "I spend every Christmas with Lady Victoria and her charming husband, Mr. Wainwright." He nodded to his cousin who had stepped ahead of him, engaging Tad in conversation while she waited for her escort. "They always have the most delicious feast. When they told me of this ball, I hadn't any interest in attending. Until I learned who our hostess would be."

Tad had bowed to Lady Victoria as she left, then he moved closer to Felicity, his gaze on the new arrival.

Before she could properly introduce them, Lord William stepped back and lifted a quizzing glass to his eye. "I must say, you've grown even more enchanting since our last meeting. Marriage must agree with you."

Her cheeks warmed and she laughed. But when Tad's eyes narrowed slightly at the exchange, Felicity awkwardly swallowed her laughter.

"I see you've not changed, Lord William," she said, her voice light but firm. "Always the flirt."

"Guilty as charged," he replied with a wink, seemingly oblivious to Tad's somber expression.

Felicity turned to her husband, her tone softening. "My love, I don't think you have met Lord William Thursby before. Though I am grateful he came to our wedding, I didn't have the chance to introduce you. Our grandmothers were quite close."

She saw a flicker of doubt in Tad's eyes, a momentary shadow that made her heart ache. She wanted to reach out, to reassure him, but the doors opened again, and more guests poured in, their kind words and compliments drawing her attention away.

"It is a pleasure, Mr. Harcourt." Lord William bowed to him with his usual easy grin. "You captured a very fine wife. Before anyone else could think to make an offer." Did she imagine the slight edge in the man's voice? What a silly notion. Lord William barely knew her. What reason would he have to show Tad any hostility?

"I am grateful every day for my good fortune," Tad answered in an even tone, his posture cold and soldier-stiff. "It is an honor to care for her."

"Indeed." Lord William's eyebrows lifted slightly, but before

Felicity could attempt any further discernment, he bowed. "I must attend to my cousin. Good evening to you both."

New guests had come into the room, giving Felicity half a moment to smile reassuringly at her husband. Though she wasn't certain *why* Tad needed reassurance. She sensed his unease as he retook his place at her side. The stream of guests continued, and Tad remained fixed beside her.

"The ball is simply marvelous, Lady Felicity, Mr. Harcourt," one lady gushed. "It reminds us all of what the Deerwoods used to do here at Winterway. You've brought life back to this place."

Felicity's heart soared at the praise, but she couldn't shake the nagging feeling that something was amiss. She glanced at Tad, his face a mask of polite attentiveness, but she could see the tension in his eyes.

The evening wore on, the music and dancing filling the room, but Felicity's mind kept drifting back to Tad, to the doubt she'd seen in his eyes, to the unspoken questions that hovered between them.

She knew she had to talk to him, to find out why Lord William's arrival had struck such a sour note, but the night was slipping away, and the demands of their guests soon necessitated that they part ways.

The evening continued to unfold with grace and merriment, guests whirling around the dance floor, laughter bubbling through the room. Felicity's heart lightened with every kind word and shared smile, her spirits lifted by the joy around her.

Then Lord William approached, his eyes alight with mischief, his hand extended in invitation. "I haven't seen you dance after you opened the ball with the rector. An interesting choice, I must say. Why not with your husband?"

"I may not be as experienced as you or your cousin, Lord William, but even I know that it is impolite for a lady to dance with her husband." She fluttered her fan before her. The room had grown warm, despite the season, and they'd started to open the windows above the heads of their guests to let the hot air escape.

"This is practically a wedding ball," her guest argued. "No one would think a thing of it, especially as you are new to the neighborhood. What would one dance hurt? If anything, it would start a mania of gossip." He waggled his eyebrows at her. "Think of all that fun."

She giggled despite herself, then hid her expression behind her fan. "I doubt my husband would find gossip about the two of us as entertaining as you would, your lordship."

He snorted. "Then we will have to change his mind. Come, Lady Felicity. May I have this dance? We can spend the whole of it talking of our late-grandmothers and confusing people who watch, as we will sure both laugh and cry throughout the experience."

Felicity glanced at Tad, who was engaged in conversation with a group of gentlemen. She knew it would be rude to refuse Lord William, and she had only danced once. She so wanted to dance again. With a gracious smile, she accepted his hand. "Of course, Lord William. Though I should like not to cry."

As they took their positions on the dance floor, Lord William's charm was in full force. He twirled her gracefully, his compliments and flattery flowing freely, making her laugh despite her reservations.

"You know, Lady Felicity," he said, his voice low and teasing, "I was quite surprised to hear of your marriage to a mere merchant. I would have thought someone of your grace and beauty would have aimed for a duke or an earl at the very least."

Felicity's laughter rang out, her amusement unfettered by what others may have thought an insult. "What earl or duke would have me? Or even know of me? Besides, a title does not a man make, my lord. My husband is kind, intelligent, and honorable. I couldn't ask for more."

Lord William's eyes twinkled, but there was a hint of something more in his gaze. "And yet, the heart wants what the heart wants. A merchant's life is far removed from what you're accustomed to."

Felicity's smile tightened, and she met his eyes squarely. "Perhaps, but it's a life I've chosen willingly, and one I'm learning to love."

He raised an eyebrow, his grin widening. "Learning to love? That doesn't sound like an endorsement."

"I didn't marry for a title, Lord William," Felicity said, her voice firm. "Such a thing is hardly important to me. I would rather have a kind husband. I would rather have companionship, partnership, something real and lasting."

"And have you found it?" he asked, his voice soft, almost tender.

Felicity's throat tightened, and she looked away, her mind filled with images of Tad, of the warmth in his eyes, the kindness in his touch. "I believe I have," she whispered, her voice filled with conviction.

Lord William was silent for a moment, then followed through the motion of the dance, stepping around and back, his eyes searching hers. "I hope so. Truly, I do."

They danced in silence for a moment, the world around them fading away. Then the music ended, and Lord William bowed, his eyes locked on hers.

"Thank you for the dance, my lady," he said, his voice tinged with something she couldn't quite identify.

"You are most welcome, Lord William," she replied, her voice steady, her eyes clear. She wanted to find Tad. To be near him. All of a sudden, she found herself missing his presence.

It did not take her long to find him, near the dance floor, speaking with an elderly couple. She sidled up next to him, immediately more at ease once at his side.

Felicity's heart filled with a mixture of pride and trepidation. She had handled Lord William's probing questions with grace, but his words had stirred something within her, something that left her feeling vulnerable. Vulnerable and . . . wistful.

She glanced at Tad, his eyes warm but distant. There were still questions to be answered, still doubts to be addressed.

But for now, she would dance, she would laugh, and she would hold her head high, knowing that she had chosen her path, and she would walk it with confidence and grace.

TAD'S GAZE HAD FOLLOWED FELICITY AS SHE DANCED with Lord William, their laughter ringing in his ears, a pang twisting in his chest. He forced himself to look away, engaging their guests. Yet the sight tugged his attention back, time and time again. Until the dance ended and his wife returned to his side with a subdued but pleasant smile.

They parted again, when she realized she had a direction to give to the head footman regarding the midnight supper. Tad watched her go, uncertainty tight in his chest. Then he turned back to Reverend Moore, who was regarding him with a kind smile.

"A splendid evening, Mr. Harcourt," the rector said, his eyes twinkling. "You and your lovely wife have outdone yourselves."

Tad managed a smile, his gratitude for the other man's words quite real. "Thank you, Reverend. My wife must have all the credit, I assure you."

"And how is married life treating you?" Reverend Moore asked, his gaze friendly but probing.

Tad's smile faltered, and he looked away, his mind a whirl of conflicting emotions. "It's . . . wonderful. Truly."

Reverend Moore's eyes softened, and he placed a reassuring hand on Tad's shoulder. "I can see that it's a new world for you, Harcourt. But have faith. Love grows in the most unexpected places, and I see an affection between you and your lady."

Tad's heart ached at the words, and he nodded, his voice barely above a whisper. "I hope so, Reverend. I truly do."

They continued to speak, the conversation turning to more mundane topics, but Tad's mind kept drifting back to Felicity, to the laughter in her eyes, to the way she had looked at Lord William. Doubts gnawed at him, doubts he couldn't shake, doubts he knew he shouldn't have.

When Felicity returned, her cheeks flushed with excitement, her eyes alight with joy, Tad's heart skipped a beat. He knew what he had to do.

"My lady," he said, his voice firm, his eyes locked on hers. "May I have the next dance?"

Her lips parted, but she said not a word. She glanced at the rector, and the pink of her cheeks darkened. It wasn't completely unheard of for a husband and wife to dance together in public, but it was a tradition that spoke to the restraint and decorum of their society. Their class.

But Tad didn't care about tradition. He didn't care about decorum. All he cared about was Felicity, about the way she looked at him, about the adoration he felt growing for her day by day.

Felicity's eyes widened, and then she smiled. A slow, beautiful smile that took his breath away. "Of course, Mr. Harcourt."

He escorted her to the newly forming lines of dancers. As they took their places on the dance floor, Tad's heart was pounding, his palms damp beneath his gloves, his mind filled with a jumble of thoughts and emotions. But as he took Felicity's hands in his, as they began to move to the music, all of that fell away.

"Is this everything you hoped for?" he asked, his voice soft as they came close, only for her ears.

Felicity's eyes sparkled, and her lips curved upward. "It's beyond everything I dreamed. Thank you for helping, for supporting this endeavor. I am a bit in awe that you would allow your bride to command such an important event."

"I have complete faith in all your abilities, my dear." He gave her hand a squeeze when they joined together again, then stepped apart. Granting him a full view of her fine figure, her beautiful new gown, her delightful grace. Was a man ever so lovesick as he felt in that moment? "I am grateful you recovered from your cold in time to enjoy all of it."

"I had a most excellent doctor," she said with a raise of her eyebrows. She arched her arm upward, and his came to meet hers.

"I aim to please," he teased, twirling her gracefully. He quite enjoyed the waltz, whatever his father had said of it being a 'scandalous thing for fashionable folk.' He couldn't imagine a better way to dance at that moment. Then he made a show of looking upward. "I still have not found my contribution to the ball. The mistletoe."

"You haven't?" She batted her eyelashes at him, all genteel surprise and innocence. "Perhaps you are not looking carefully enough."

He affected what he hoped passed as a tragic expression, and she giggled. "Alas, I will have to live without a kiss this night. A sorry fate, indeed."

"Do you want a hint?"

"Will you think less of me for needing one?"

"Most likely not."

"Hm. But dare I risk such a thing?" Already he risked so much, loving her as he did, without reserve. Without knowing how she felt. Linked to her forever, and unaware if she would rejoice when she learned of his feelings. "Best not," he said at last. "Though I promise I will not give up the search. Even if it takes me all winter to find it."

"Let us hope not." She lowered her gaze momentarily. "Or let us hope that you will not need mistletoe to justify a kiss or two for your wife."

His heart thrummed happily at that. "I need naught but my wife's permission to allow such a thing."

"Really?" Her gaze met his and she lowered her lashes. "You have it, you know. My most enthusiastic permission."

Tad's ears ceased hearing the music. "That seems a dangerous thing to grant in the middle of a crowded ballroom. What if I wished a kiss at this very moment?"

She lifted her chin and leaned closer than the steps of the dance required as they stood, waiting for another couple to prance around the two of them. Oblivious to everything but each other. "It may scandalize your guests, Mr. Harcourt, but it would not scandalize *me*." He'd never seen her so bold, had he?

The room hadn't been so warm a moment ago, surely?

The music, the enjoyment of the evening, had granted her courage, it would seem. He had to swallow back the very strong urge to take her up on the offer. Dancing with her would cause enough of the stuffier people present to gossip. But kissing his wife, in public? They would be the talk of the town for ages.

"I had better wait for the mistletoe," he whispered, then stepped back into the formation of the dance. The air around him cooled, but he felt warmer beneath his cravat than he had ever on a summer's day.

She didn't look disappointed, but instead most satisfied. "Spoilsport," she whispered.

He shook his head. "I must restrict myself to the movements the dance calls for, my lady. I fear anything more will lower your opinion of me as a partner."

"Unlikely," she returned as she wove around another couple to rejoin him, taking his arm around her as they walked forward. "You are by far my favorite partner in the history of my life."

"That cannot be." He hardly knew what he was doing anymore with his feet. His hands only obeyed the set steps because it meant touching and holding Felicity. "And what of your dance with Lord William? I saw the way he led you across the floor. Quite expertly."

Her laugh blended with the music, a gentle reminder of what drew him to her. "Lord William is a fine dancer, but . . ." Her voice trailed off as she met his eyes, a warmth in her gaze. "You, Tad, are the one I would choose every time to partner with." The earnest light in her hazel eyes touched every corner of his heart, clearing the shadows of his doubt quite thoroughly. "I much prefer dancing with you."

He very much wished everyone else would go home at that instant.

All that mattered was her, the feel of her hands in his, the warmth of her smile, the look in her eyes. A look, he thought, filled with something that felt suspiciously like love. And as they came to the end of the dance, Tad hoped, with his whole soul, that he'd interpreted her words and her look correctly.

She loved him.

The dance ended, but the connection lingered, a warmth in Tad's chest that he never wanted to lose. Reluctantly, they parted to mingle with their guests, their eyes meeting across the room, a shared understanding passing between them.

As the hours wore on, the ballroom buzzed with conversation, the music a continuous melody that filled the room. Tad found himself lost in the whirlwind of the evening, the joy and excitement infectious, but his thoughts kept returning to Felicity, to the way she had looked in his arms, to the softness in her eyes.

He couldn't find the mistletoe. But even if he had found it in the middle of the ballroom, nothing would have stopped him from kissing her. From showing her, and everyone else, how deeply he loved her.

Finally, as the clock struck two, the last guests departed, leaving Tad and Felicity standing in the empty foyer, exhaustion etching his wife's beautiful face, but triumph in her eyes.

"You were incredible," Tad said when the door shut for the last time. The footmen faded away, leaving the couple completely alone. He pulled Felicity into his arms, his voice filled with awe and pride. "This night was a success, all thanks to you."

Felicity looked up at him, a shy smile playing on her lips. "I couldn't have done it without you."

Tad's heart swelled, and he kissed her forehead, his lips brushing her skin as he spoke. "You are amazing, Felicity. Truly. I am so proud to be your husband."

She blushed, her gaze dropping to the floor, but her smile widened. "And I am proud to be your wife."

They stood in silence for a moment, the weight of the evening settling on him, the reality of his feelings sinking deeply into his heart. Tad could feel the pull of his own bed, the lure of sleep, but he knew that he couldn't leave Felicity, not now, not tonight.

"Tad?" she said, her voice soft, almost hesitant. "Would you . . . would you spend what is left of the night with me? In my bed?"

Tad's heart stopped, and he looked at her, his eyes wide, his mind a whirl of thoughts and emotions. She hadn't been the one to ask before. He'd asked her. Had knocked on the door. Had waited on her agreement. Hadn't touched her beyond what he'd asked for the first time they shared her bed. It was the same, yet entirely different, for her to invite him there. It was a new intimacy, a step forward in their relationship.

And he knew, without a doubt, that he wanted to take that step.

"Of course," he whispered, his voice thick with emotion. "I would be honored."

She smiled, her eyes filled with relief and happiness, and she took his hand, leading him deeper into their home. As they walked, Tad's mind was a blur, his heart pounding in his chest, his body filled with a longing and a desire that he had never felt before.

He knew that tonight was a turning point, a moment that would define their relationship, a moment that would bring them closer together. And as they entered Felicity's room, Tad knew that he was ready for whatever came next.

For he was in love with his wife, and he knew, with a certainty that filled him with joy and wonder, that she was in love with him too.

Seventeen

Felicity lay on her side, her eyes fixed on Tad as he slept beside her, his chest rising and falling in a gentle rhythm. They had been too tired, too spent from the previous night's festivities to do anything but fall into a deep, contented sleep, their bodies entwined, their hearts full.

But now, as she watched him, as she studied the lines of his face and the curve of his lips, Felicity's heart ached with a longing, a desire that she hadn't allowed herself to fully acknowledge before. She wanted him. She wanted to be his, completely and utterly, in every way.

She reached out, her hand trembling slightly, and brushed a stray lock of dark hair from his forehead, her fingers light on his skin. Her mind raced, her thoughts a jumble of uncertainty and fear. How could she tell him? How could she express what she was feeling without sounding foolish or naive? Worse yet, what if he rejected her? What if he didn't want her in the way she wanted him?

Her fears were interrupted as Tad's hand suddenly caught hers, his eyes fluttering open, his gaze locking with hers. He smiled, a soft, knowing smile, and brought her fingers to his lips, kissing them gently.

"You're awake," she whispered, her voice catching in her throat.

"I have been for a while," he replied, his voice low and warm. "I've been watching you."

She blushed, a thrill running through her at the thought of him watching over her, or perhaps even admiring her as she slept. "You have?"

He nodded, his eyes never leaving hers. "You are beautiful, Felicity. I couldn't help myself."

Her heart skipped a beat, and her shyness gave way to a newfound confidence. "You are not so terrible to look at either, Mr. Harcourt."

He laughed, the sound rich and deep, and he pulled her closer, his arms wrapping around her. "I'm glad you think so."

They lay in silence for a moment, the warmth of their bodies a comfort, the intimacy of their connection a joy. Felicity's mind still whirled, but she knew that she could trust him, that she could open her heart to him. That she could take the next step.

"Tad," she said, her voice soft and full of emotion. "I want to tell you something."

"Hm?" His hand smoothed away the loose curls around her face. He looked at her, his eyes filled with tenderness. "What is it, my love?"

That single word made confidence surge through her heart.

She took a deep breath, gathering her courage, her words a whisper. "I love you, Tad. With everything I am."

His eyes widened, and he looked at her, his face filled with wonder and awe. "Felicity . . ."

"I love you," she repeated, her voice filled with conviction, her heart laid bare. "I want to be your wife, in every way. Completely and utterly yours."

He was silent for a moment, his eyes searching hers, while she fought to keep uncertainty at bay. Waited, impatiently, for his reassurance. He loved her too. She knew he did. She'd seen it already, in a thousand tiny ways, that he'd given her his heart.

At last he released a soft, trembling laugh. Then a smile that lit up his face and filled her with joy.

"I love you too, Felicity," he whispered, his voice filled with emotion. "And I want to be your husband, in every way."

"Then you had best look up," she said, tears of happiness in her eyes.

Her husband's eyebrows came together sharply, the confusion in his eyes adorable. He obliged her, glancing upward. When his eyes caught sight of the mistletoe she had hung there the night before, tied to the canopy above where they held each other, a laugh rumbled in his chest and came out in a burst of relief.

"Oh, my darling wife." He didn't waste another word, another breath, another moment, before kissing her quite soundly.

And she knew, with a certainty that filled her with peace, that they were ready. Ready to take the next step, ready to be one, ready to face whatever came next.

Together.

Eighteen

CHRISTMAS DAY

Tad awoke with the dawn, a smile hovering on his lips as he glanced over at Felicity, still peacefully lost in dreams. Her face was serene, a soft smile playing at her lips, as though her sleeping hours were as pleasant as his waking reality. The temptation to reach out, to caress her cheek, nearly overwhelmed him, but he resisted. Today was a special day, and he had plans.

Quietly, he slipped out of the bed, leaving Felicity wrapped in the warmth of their shared blankets. He knew exactly how he wanted this Christmas morning to unfold. His heart was light, his spirit buoyed by a happiness he'd never known before. Marriage had brought him not only a partner but a companion, a friend, a confidante. And with each passing day, the bond between them grew, their affection deepening into something profound.

He went to the drapes and pulled them aside enough to look out at the sky, hoping the weather would cooperate with his plans. Clear blue sky stretched overhead, and he immediately relaxed. As he turned, the painting hanging above the fireplace caught his eye, lit as it was by the sunlight he'd allowed in through the window.

The painting came alive with the fresh glow of Christmas morning, a scene imbued with an almost magical quality. Each snow-laden rooftop in the village sparkled with a delicate frosting of ice, reflecting the bright rays of the morning sun. The cobblestone streets, painted with a soft and gentle hand, lay covered in a pristine blanket of snow, untouched except for the faint trails of a few early risers.

Children with flushed cheeks and bright eyes were depicted, their laughter frozen in time as they playfully engaged in snow-ball fights or built cheerful snowmen at the edge of the village green.

In the distance, the church's steeple reached towards the clear, blue sky. Its windows gleamed with a warm and inviting glow, promising shelter and camaraderie within. Each cottage in the painting exuded a sense of home and hearth, with smoke lazily billowing from the chimneys, hinting at the cozy fires and joyful gatherings taking place inside.

Everything about the scene depicted seemed as though it had come from his hopes and dreams for that Christmas day, and he took confidence from the beauty and brightness depicted in the painted version of Lynford Hollow. Their new home.

With a last, loving look at his slumbering wife, Tad crept from the room, excitement bubbling within him.

He had barely slept, his mind far too busy with thoughts of the day ahead. His gift for Felicity would arrive today. Until then, he wanted to make the day one to remember. The morning was theirs, a private celebration of their first Christmas as husband and wife.

He'd arranged a surprise, something he hoped would delight Felicity and add a touch of magic to the day. Outside the kitchen, he waited for Cook and Clara to prepare a breakfast tray. The maid handed it to him with a delighted grin.

He added a sprig of mistletoe, another he had saved from his expedition into the trees, beside the plate for a festive touch. Then, tray in hand, he made his way back to Felicity's bedchamber.

Felicity's eyes fluttered open as he entered, surprise in her gaze as she took in the sight of him bearing breakfast. Her smile was like the sun breaking through the clouds, and his heart swelled with affection.

"Happy Christmas, my love," he said, placing the tray on her lap.

Her eyes sparkled as she took in the holly, the details of the meal he had put so much thought into. "Tad, this is wonderful. You didn't have to bring me breakfast."

"A special day deserves a special start," he replied, his voice filled with warmth. "And after breakfast, you must dress warmly. I've been informed the pond is ready for skating."

"Oh, I haven't skated in ages." Her expression softened. "I'm afraid I cannot today, either. I no longer have a pair of skates." The wistful, sad expression on her face would have torn his heart in two had he not prepared for this exact moment.

With a triumphant smile, he pulled a box from beneath the bed and presented it to her. "Your first Christmas gift," he said, not disguising his pleasure.

Tears welled in her eyes as she opened the box to reveal the skates, her hands trembling as she touched the blades. "Oh, Tad," she whispered, her voice thick with emotion.

"Clara stole your boots for me, so the smithy could make certain the blades and straps would fit them correctly."

"They're perfect."

He leaned in and kissed her soundly, tasting her happiness,

feeling her joy. "I thought you might like them. And I thought it was due time we become sensations together out on the ice."

"You thought correctly," she breathed, her eyes shining with love and gratitude. "Thank you, Tad. This is the most wonderful Christmas ever."

With a final, adoring kiss, he left her to enjoy her breakfast, his heart filled with a contentment he'd never known. They were building a life together, and it was more beautiful than he'd ever dared to imagine.

And this was only the start.

The air was crisp and clear as Tad and Felicity made their way to the pond, tucked beneath a thick blanket in their sleigh. The world around them was a winter wonderland, the country-side blanketed in a layer of pristine snow that sparkled in the morning sun. Her excitement was infectious as he guided the horses with practiced ease.

Felicity's cheeks were flushed with cold, her eyes shining with anticipation. The joy of the day had awakened a childlike delight within both of them, and Tad found himself looking forward to the simple pleasure of gliding across the ice.

As they neared the pond, the sound of laughter and shouts of glee reached their ears. A group of children were already enjoying the ice, their faces rosy and bright as they skated and played. Some were even pushing younger siblings about in sledges, their laughter ringing through the cold air.

Tad brought the sleigh to a stop, and they climbed down, the children's eyes widening as they recognized Tad and Felicity from their recent snowman-building adventure. Several of them skated over, their faces alight with smiles.

"Mr. Harcourt! Lady Felicity!" they shouted, their voices bubbling with excitement. "Will you skate with us?"

Tad's grin was broad as he helped Felicity attach the blades to her boots. "Indeed we will," he said, his voice filled with cheer. "In fact, what do you say we have some races?"

The children's cheers were deafening, but it was Felicity's wide grin that made his heart soar with joy. How could he ever worry again, or doubt anything, in the face of her happiness?

Tad helped his wife strap on her skates before seeing to his own, buckling the newly sharpened blades to his sturdy winter boots. Then he led her out onto the frozen pond, her movements a bit uncertain at first, but quickly growing more confident. The children were fearless, their laughter filling the air as they darted past, challenging Tad and Felicity to keep up.

Tad raced beside his wife, feeling more alive than he could ever remember. The world fell away as they skated, the cold air filled with children's laughter.

They raced and played, the children's energy boundless. Tad and Felicity lost themselves in the moment, the worries and cares of adulthood forgotten in the face of such pure, unbridled happiness.

As the sun climbed higher in the sky, Tad finally called a halt, his breath misting in the air as he laughed and took his wife in his embrace at the center of the pond.

"I believe we've been thoroughly bested," he declared, his voice warm with affection.

Felicity's laughter rang out, her heart full to bursting. "Indeed we have," she agreed, her eyes meeting Tad's. "I think they could last hours more, and here I am longing for tea and a nap. But I wouldn't have it any other way."

They said their goodbyes to the children, their hearts light, their spirits buoyed by the joy of the day. As they made their way back to the sleigh, Felicity's hand tucked into Tad's arm, he knew that this was a Christmas they would remember forever. It certainly was his favorite Christmas with Felicity by his side.

Tad felt a warmth in his chest, watching Felicity's eyes sparkle with the day's joyous escapades. "Can we do this every Christmas?" she asked.

He chuckled. "Why limit ourselves to just Christmas? I'd take you to that pond every day if it makes you this happy."

She kept close to him the whole ride home, speaking rapidly of her enjoyment of the day and observations involving the village children. His heart was full to bursting with love for the woman at his side. She could ask anything of him in that moment and he'd gladly oblige. It amazed him that she still seemed surprised by his devotion.

When they'd agreed to this marriage, he'd promised himself he'd ensure her happiness. And in their short time together, she'd brought him immeasurable joy.

As he guided her inside their house, the winter's chill flushed his cheeks, making his eyes feel alive. The study was warm and inviting. Together, they shed their damp clothes, placing them by the fire. He caught her watching him as he stoked the flames, and he felt a surge of pride. How he'd managed to earn such affection from this wonderful woman was beyond his understanding.

Settling onto the sofa, he opened his arms, inviting her in. The feel of her against him, so close and intimate, made his heart race. The firelight reflected in her eyes, making them glow.

"Felicity," he began, voice laden with emotion, "today was incredible beyond words. Having you by my side made it unforgettable."

Her response warmed him even more. "I've never been so happy," she whispered.

He gently brushed a stray curl from her face, losing himself in her gaze. Their lips met, and the world faded away. He could have remained in that moment forever.

Suddenly, she pulled away, her face a picture of distress. "Tad, I'm a horrible wife."

He frowned, taken aback. "What? Why?"

"Since the moment you woke up, you've been doing kind things for me, giving me gifts. I have something for you, too, and I nearly forgot."

Her confession about forgetting his gift brought a smirk to his face. He couldn't resist teasing her. "Do you find me that distracting?"

She huffed and stood. "My, but you are confident." She pretended to glare at him, but he affected a look of innocence until it finally made her laugh. "Yes, I suppose I do find you 'that distracting.' Do you want your present or not?"

He didn't even try to hide his adoration as he said, "As you are the giver, then yes. Please, Felicity."

"Thankfully, I needn't go far for it." She went to the hearth where a small, decorative music box perched. When she opened it, he smiled at the music. Music he would never tire of hearing because it now meant he was home. With his wife. She lifted out a small, brown paper wrapped parcel.

Tad's eyes widened when she turned, and a playful grin spread across her face.

"How long has that been there?"

"Long enough," she teased. "Directly under your nose." She handed him the neatly wrapped package, her hands trembling as their fingers brushed. Was she nervous?

"I hope you like it," she whispered.

Tad's hands were gentle as he unwrapped the gift, his gaze hardly leaving hers. Inside he found a finely crafted pocket watch, the casing engraved with intricate designs of ships. The pocket watch was exquisite, and the thought behind it made it even more special.

His heart swelled.

Tad was at a loss for words. All he could do was pull her close, his voice thick with emotion. "This is perfect, Felicity. It's a constant reminder of the time we've shared and the moments yet to come. Thank you, my love."

Silently, he vowed that he would never take a single of those moments, the days, the hours, the minutes, not even the seconds with her, for granted.

They sat together by the fire, their arms around each other, their hearts beating as one. The world outside could have ceased to exist as they lost themselves in each other, the warmth of the fire reflecting the warmth of their love.

AS THE AFTERNOON WORE ON, FELICITY'S EXCITEMENT softened into a joyful contentment. The day had been perfect. The memories of their first Christmas together would remain with her for the rest of her life, marking the day as one of wonder.

She was about to suggest she and Tad leave their book and dress for dinner when a loud knock echoed throughout the house. She blinked up at her husband, whose arm had rested around her waist while he held their book in his other hand.

"Who could that be?"

Tad raised his eyebrows. "We had better go see, hadn't we?" He took her hand and squeezed it reassuringly. "It seems the surprises of the day are not yet over."

She narrowed her eyes at him and poked him in the rib, making him chuckle. "You are behaving suspiciously, my love."

"Am I?" He kissed her forehead tenderly. "Come. We ought to hurry before our guests give up and return home."

"We really do have guests?" She darted to her feet. "I hope someone let them in." She hurried to the entrance, Tad close behind her.

One of the footmen had, thankfully, let their guests inside.

Mr. and Mrs. Moore were removing their winter things when Felicity rushed forward. "Our dear friends! Goodness, I didn't know you were coming. Are you here for dinner? Please say you are."

"Of course we're here for dinner," Eliza said, her voice filled with amusement. "Goodness. I knew we were bringing you a surprise from your husband, but not that we were a surprise as well."

"Clever chap," Mr. Moore said as he bent down to pick up a box. He'd likely put it down while removing his overcoat. "Happy Christmas to you both."

"Thank you," Tad said, his arm going around her shoulder. "And thank you for bringing that." He nodded to the box. "It wasn't any trouble, I hope?"

"None at all." Mr. Moore rocked back on his heels as Felicity looked between the two of them with curiosity. "Young Jeremiah assured me he picked the very best for Lady Felicity."

"The very best what?" she asked, looking to Eliza for an explanation since the men didn't seem eager to give one.

"You will see." Eliza's eyes twinkled with mischief.

"Come. Let us return to the fire." Tad released her long enough to lead the way back into the warmth of the room they'd left behind, and Eliza took Felicity's arm to tell her excitedly of her own happy Christmas morning.

Mr. Moore, Felicity noted, carried the box carefully. As if it contained something precious.

Once they had settled into the drawing room, Felicity's curiosity got the better of her, and she glanced once more at the box in the vicar's hands. Before she could ask, he handed it to Tad.

"Jeremiah promised it is exactly what you asked for," Mr. Moore told her husband, his voice filled with a knowing delight.

Tad's eyes sparkled as he turned to Felicity, holding the box out to her. "Another Christmas gift for you, my love."

Surprise made Felicity's mouth pop open. "Oh, but—you already gave me a gift."

"I know," her husband said, stilling grinning at her.

"Best open it, dear," Eliza said with a gentle smile.

Felicity took the box with trembling hands. As she opened it, a tiny meow escaped, and her eyes widened in disbelief. Nestled inside was a small, adorable, gray-striped kitten, its eyes wide and curious as it stared up at her.

Tears welled in Felicity's eyes as she carefully lifted the kitten out of the box, cuddling it close. It purred contentedly, nestling against her neck as if it already knew it had found its home.

When she looked at her husband, feeling a mixture of disbelief and gratitude, Tad explained the kitten with a gentleness in his voice. "I remembered the story you told me about the kitten you received when you were a girl. I hoped this little one could bring you joy, just as that one did."

"Oh, Tad," she whispered, her voice choked with emotion. "This is the most thoughtful gift. Thank you."

Tad reached out, brushing a tear from her cheek, his own eyes filled with tenderness. "Anything to make you happy, Felicity. Anything at all."

The rest of the evening was filled with laughter and joy as they celebrated Christmas together with the Moores. The house was filled with the warmth of friendship, the comfort of shared traditions, and the promise of a bright and loving future.

Felicity had found her place, not just as Tad's wife but as a cherished member of a community that welcomed her with open arms.

As the night wore on, she glanced over at Tad, his eyes meeting hers across the room. In his gaze, she saw the reflection of her own happiness, her own love, and she knew that they were on the path to something truly wonderful.

Together, they were building a life, a love, and a legacy that would endure, nourished by the shared understanding and deep connection that only true love could bring.

Felicity felt a profound sense of happiness, her heart full of love for her husband, her new family, and the little kitten that symbolized so much more than a mere gift. It was a testament to Tad's attentiveness, his love, and his desire to make her happy in every way. The little kitten curled up in her lap, and she knew that this Christmas would be one she would cherish forever.

Epilogue

NEW YEAR'S DAY

F elicity and Tad had stayed at home the evening before, though a few of their neighbors had invited them to ring in the New Year at dinner parties. There would be time aplenty for getting to know their neighbors better, but it was the first time the two of them would greet a new year together. Though they hadn't done anything particularly important, Felicity had enjoyed every moment of her evening.

They'd spent the hours after dinner in the drawing room, rearranging furniture of all things. Laughing and teasing one another as they had nonsense conversations about the best placement of a chair or cushion.

They'd even gone about the house moving the art on the walls around, together. And Felicity's kitten followed them, darting between their legs and being an adorable nuisance. Felicity had asked Tad to carry the painting from her room, where only she and he enjoyed it, to the drawing room.

"I want anyone who comes into our home to see how important the village is to us. How important our friends and neighbors are," she had said. Tad had agreed and put the picture above the mantel with the help of a surprised footman.

This morning, Felicity nestled comfortably on the plush sofa before the hearth in the drawing room. On her lap, her gray tabby kitten pounced at a dangling ribbon she held, its tiny paws batting with innocent enthusiasm.

Beside her, Tad sat with an arm draped protectively around her shoulders.

"Have you thought of a name for the little beast yet?"

She shook her head. "I keep thinking we ought to name her something ladylike, but then she gives me such a fierce look that perhaps something with more dash would be appropriate."

"I cannot think there are many people who would think a kitten in need of a dashing name."

She let the kitten get hold of the ribbon, then the cat took the prize and jumped to the floor, tumbling onto its back to wrestle more with the strip of silk.

"Perhaps I'll name her Tiger."

Tad kissed her forehead as she rested it against his shoulder. "What does your cousin say?"

In his free hand, he held a letter received the day before, from a cousin on his mother's side. Her eyes studied his contented expression rather than the elegant handwriting as Tad read aloud.

"'I hope you are settling into both your new home and married life with happiness. I can think you deserve nothing less. Your mother has said Lady Felicity is a lovely, charming person who writes excellent letters. If I send her one, do you think she will find it impertinent?'"

Felicity released a soft snort. "Of course not. I adore letters. In fact, I will send her one tomorrow. Which cousin is this?"

"Eleanor Blanding. The eldest child of my mother's younger brother."

"Do you have a lot of cousins?"

"Mother came from a large family," he said with a shrug. "I think I have fifteen first cousins on her side."

"Fifteen?" Felicity pulled in a soft gasp. "You never said there were that many of them."

"We hadn't talked of my cousins before." He tilted his head to look down at her with raised eyebrows. "Is the number important?"

"Yes!" Felicity sat, a sense of excitement building in her. "Because they are my cousins now, too."

Her husband's eyes widened somewhat. "They would be, yes." Then his lips turned upward. "You missed having family."

"Terribly." It didn't hurt as much, remembering the years of being without her parents, living alone with her grandmother. She would always miss them. With Tad in her life, the pain had eased. He was her family. Their new home provided friends and a community.

To have cousins on top of the rest was an unlooked for gift.

"Can we invite them to visit?"

"What? All fifteen of them?" Tad's forehead wrinkled. "I'm not certain we have enough guest rooms, but if you wish it, we can work it out—"

She placed her hand over his heart, interrupting him gently. "You wonderful, dear man. It needn't happen all at once," she said. "Having a few people at a time to visit would be lovely. I want to get to know all of them."

Tad folded the letter and placed it on the other side of the couch, then wrapped Felicity in both his arms and pulled her closer. "Anything you wish, Felicity. We will have as many cousins, aunts, uncles, and the like to visit us here, as often as you like. But will you promise me something? Do save a little of your time just for me."

"Of course." She tipped her head back enough to kiss his jawline. "You will always be my favorite."

"That is a relief to know."

"I especially want to have family for Christmas next year." She watched the kitten yawn and curl up on the rug before the fire. Tired from all its play. "I can't help but hope we can bring the same joy we've found here to others."

Tad nodded in agreement, his gaze warm when she turned to meet it. "I think that's a wonderful idea."

"We could have Eleanor come."

"And her sisters. She has two. I suppose we might even invite my aunt and uncle." Tad's teasing smile didn't dissuade her in the slightest.

Felicity nodded rapidly. "That would be lovely! And perhaps some of my grandmother's old friends, and mine. I was also thinking of one more person we ought to invite."

Tad looked at her inquisitively. "Oh? Who did you have in mind?"

She hesitated for a moment, choosing her words carefully. "Well...I thought perhaps Lord William might join us. With Lady Victoria as his only reason to visit the neighborhood, I doubt we'd see him often otherwise. And I feel that he might appreciate having some friends."

Tad's surprise was evident, but he spoke without judgement. "Why Lord William?"

"I think he's a good man, Tad. The way he cared about his grandmother, and coming to our wedding was a kind gesture, too. I wonder if he was as lonely as I was. Lady Victoria's company isn't exactly a comfort to anyone." She winced somewhat.

After a moment of studying her, Tad's expression softened. "If you believe he deserves our company and friendship, I trust your judgment."

Felicity smiled gratefully, then kissed his cheek. "Thank you, Tad. Your understanding and trust mean the world to me."

Tad leaned in, pressing a gentle kiss to her forehead. "Anything for you, my love."

"Anything? But, Tad, I have you. I need nothing else."

He laughed and kissed her, pressing his lips to hers with such tenderness and love that everything inside her went warm and soft. She twined her arms around his shoulders and threaded her fingers through his hair. Though a novice at the practice, she'd grown very fond of kissing of her husband.

When they parted, Tad rested his forehead against hers. "Perhaps we can wait a month or so to invite anyone to visit?"

"You want me all to yourself, do you?"

"In this one thing, I'm very selfish."

She gave him a brief kiss. "I will give you my undivided attention for a month then. After that, I want to flood this house with family."

He raised his eyebrows higher. "You know, my love, there are other sorts of family. Would you like sons and daughters, as well as cousins-in-law? We can begin the work of inviting that sort of family at this moment, if you wish."

The way her stomach flipped and heat flooded her cheeks made her gasp. "*Theodore Harcourt.*"

He grinned and kissed her senseless.

Above the mantel, through one of the painting's cottage windows, the outline of a delicate wooden cradle appeared. In the warmth of the glowing hearth, it waited to welcome someone new. Neither Tad nor Felicity noticed.

But they would. When the time was right.

DID YOU ENJOY TAD AND FELICITY'S STORY? THERE IS SO much more to come. Perhaps even a future visit from the mysterious Mr. and Mrs. Deerwood.

Don't miss a thing when you sign up for Sally Britton's news on her website.

If you'd like more wintry romance this very instant, try Sally Britton's Regency novella: *The Captain and Miss Winter.*

You can also support the author by purchasing books directly from her site at authorsallybritton.store. This includes ebooks, audiobooks, and print.

Also by Sally Britton

About the Author

I'm Sally Britton, and I live in Oklahoma with my husband and our four incredible children. Our household is complete with two Australian Shepherds, a Queen Tabby Cat, and our Ball Python named Basil.

I write Regency romance primarily because my favorite author in that genre hasn't published a book in years. Over two-hundred, to be precise. And while I don't claim to be as good as Jane Austen, I certainly do my best to instill a love for her world in my books, and the hope of romance in every single page.

I began my writing journey in my teenage years, crafting my first story on my mother's electric typewriter at the age of fourteen. Immersing myself in the works of authors like Jane Austen, Louisa May Alcott, and Lucy Maud Montgomery, I felt drawn to create stories set in the elegant and complex worlds of centuries past. Among these tales, my favorite moments were always the declarations of love by the heroines, and it became evident that all of my books would center around these romantic themes.

In 2007, I earned my bachelor's degree in English with a focus on British literature. Not long after, I met and married my husband, and together we've been building our own happily ever after.

The quote, "What is done in love is done well," attributed to Vincent Van Gogh, has become my personal motto. It guides both my life and the stories I write. I believe in crafting narratives where expressing love is an act of bravery, and where kindness consistently emerges as the right choice.

If you'd like to connect with me and stay updated, you can visit my website at AuthorSallyBritton.com. I also actively engage with readers on Instagram (@authorsallybritton) and have a fan group on Facebook.

Made in the USA
Middletown, DE
27 November 2023

43728443R00110